SOUTH

SOUTH

a novel

RARE MACHINES

Babak Lakghomi

Publisher: Kwame Scott Fraser | Acquiring editor: Russell Smith
Cover designer: Laura Boyle
Cover image: type: Laura Boyle; lake: istock.com/vvvita

Library and Archives Canada Cataloguing in Publication

Title: South : a novel / Babak Lakghomi.
Names: Lakghomi, Babak, author.
Identifiers: Canadiana (print) 20220435618 | Canadiana (ebook) 20220435693 | ISBN 9781459750814 (softcover) | ISBN 9781459750838 (EPUB) | ISBN 9781459750821 (PDF)
Classification: LCC PS8623.A4225 S68 2023 | DDC C813/.6—dc23

We acknowledge the support of the Canada Council for the Arts and the Ontario Arts Council for our publishing program. We also acknowledge the financial support of the Government of Ontario, through the Ontario Book Publishing Tax Credit and Ontario Creates, and the Government of Canada.

Rare Machines, an imprint of Dundurn Press
1382 Queen Street East
Toronto, Ontario, Canada M4L 1C9
dundurn.com, @dundurnpress

For Gian

CHAPTER 1

I'd decided to drive instead of taking a plane to the South. I watched the sky turn red, the dunes deform and reshape. There were fewer cars the farther south I drove. The condition of the roads became worse.

Occasionally, a dilapidated gas station on the way. I filled up with gas and purchased water. Other than that, no sign of towns or villages. The cashiers looked surprised to see a car other than trucks loaded with machinery on that road.

At night I stopped the car by the roadside to sleep. The desert night was cold. I no longer had any phone coverage.

Putting up my tent and slipping into my sleeping bag reminded me of being with Tara. We would've had a campfire if she were here. How quickly she'd set it. Her hands snapping the twigs, piling the dry branches. Her hair long and damp. The thorns sizzling. The smell of pine leaves when she'd blow into the fire.

I was still cold in the flimsy sleeping bag. The wind flapped the tent cover and I could hear the layers of the deep rock crack beneath the sand. I listened to the strange music of the earth until I fell asleep.

When I woke up the next day, the tent was covered in sand.

My back ached. I left my tent, cleared the sand that piled over the car with my hands.

The corpse of a dead bird by the tent. Lost its way, got trapped in the desert.

I went back inside the car. I turned up the heat, rubbed my hands together, ate cold red beans out of a tin can.

I had felt connected to Tara again right before departing, but now, as I ate this cold meal in silence, she seemed like a memory from the far past.

Here I was in the middle of nowhere. Yet I had hoped this would be the kind of trip that would help change things.

I laughed at the idea myself, at being naive enough to suppress my numerous doubts about the trip.

I packed my sleeping bag and disassembled the tent. The wind blew. It made folding the tent hard. It took me a while to get back on the main road again.

I continued driving. Dried-out streams, sun-burnt palms. Tiny bugs hit the windshield and left yellow stains on the glass.

Once in a while, I'd pass a truck loaded with pumps, valves, or pipes. A sleepy driver trying to keep his eyes on the road.

The wind swirled the sand around. A black crow pecked at something by the side of the road.

After several hours of driving, signs of a village appeared in the distance. I could smell salt, the sweetness of the date trees.

I slowed down through the narrow alleys with walls made of clay. Kids ran after my car, shouting through the cloud of dust, waving their hands.

"Room, room," they'd shout. They were offering to take me to a shelter.

I slowed the car, and one of the boys overtook the others. I stopped, rolled down the window. The other boys looked at him with envy. I asked him to jump in. He kept talking to me in a dialect I could barely understand, pointing his finger at the turns.

I heard "wind" and "bread" among his words. I heard "water" and "drought."

Salt was inseparable from the soil. Cows soaked in shallow saline waters to get away from the heat. The tops of their coats burned under the sun. Patches of red, wounded flesh. Stains of salt on their backs. They lowed with a sound I'd not heard before.

When I got to the house, the boy's father was ready to receive me as if he'd already known about my arrival. I wondered if many people passed through the village. I gave the boy a small tip and paid the deposit to the father. I was told that I could pay for the food and the room when I left.

The father showed me a fish inside a bucket filled with ice. "Baby shark," he said.

We were still kilometres away from the sea, from the fishing boats, from where pearl hunters dived down deep, holding their breath for minutes at a time.

When I asked where the fish was from, the father laughed, curling his thick lips, showing his missing front teeth.

An hour later, the father gutted the fish in front of me. Stray dogs circled, hoping to get something. The father added wood to the fire, boiled the fish inside a pot. I watched the sons and the father around the fire before going to my room, their faces red in the firelight.

The boy brought me my dinner on a metal tray, showed me my futon. He pushed his drooling baby brother out of the room and shut the door. The baby kept crying and scratching the door from the other side, like a cat. There was no fork to eat with. The fish was served with yellow rice.

I remembered the father's hands gutting the fish. The wounded backs of the cows.

The aroma of the spices filled the room. I took several bites, using my hands to eat, but couldn't eat much. I washed my hands in the bowl of water in the corner of the room. I opened the door and pushed the tray outside, then quickly shut the door to keep the little boy out.

The bedsheets smelled of camphor. I was anxious that I wouldn't be able to sleep despite being tired. I was sensitive to new places, new smells. My sleeping had been worse since I had stopped drinking.

My neck was sore from the long drive and spending the previous night in the sleeping bag. I craved a hot shower. The boy had suggested that he could bring me some hot water to wash myself, but it wasn't the same as a shower. I didn't feel good about using their limited fresh water.

I took a muscle relaxant and a sleeping pill, gulped the pills down with some water. I don't know how long it took me to go to sleep.

In my sleep, I heard laughter. I woke up, or thought I did. I felt the laughter getting closer, as if it was merely coming from inside my head. I tried to scream.

I woke up drenched in sweat, my mouth dry, like I'd been eating sand.

Outside, the sound of drums. The flames of a fire lit the room through the window.

I drank water from a clay cup left by my side. I left my futon and opened the door.

In the other room, the boy and his brothers were asleep on the floor beside their mother. The father's futon was empty, but traces of his body were visible on the sheets.

I tiptoed through their bodies, left the house, and walked toward the fire.

They hit their drums. Bamboo sticks cut the hot air. Men wearing white clothes moved their bodies to the sound. They circled a man on his knees.

Women in veils looked like crows with metal beaks. One of them carried a plate of burning charcoal. Her right hand circulated the smoke, distributed it among the crowd.

Platters with bowls of rosewater, wild rue, dates around the fire.

The woman sprinkled rosewater on the sitting man's face, rubbed ash on his forehead.

The boy's father was standing among the other people. He held a chicken by its neck, a machete in his other hand.

The smell of wild rue and incense. Blood splashing, spilling into rosewater.

I sat on the sand, several metres away from the crowd.

They dipped their bamboo sticks in blood.

"People of the wind," they sang.

They threw a white cloth over the sitting man's head and struck their drums.

"When a body is sick," they sang.

"When the soul is weak."

The drums beat harder. A man blew into his pipe.

"The wind is waiting."

"They ride on the winds."

"They come from the sea."

The man convulsed under the cloth. When he started to scream, the drums stopped. His scream made something thump inside my ears.

The boy's father drew the cloth away from the man's face, held the man's head in both his hands, stared at his eyes. He pulled the man's neck toward himself and hit him in the back with his stick.

"Leave," the father shouted. "Leave us," he whispered.

When the man stopped convulsing, the father caressed his head. The father walked around, looking into everybody's eyes, sprinkling water on their faces.

"Beware of the south winds," he said when he came by my side. He rubbed the palm of his hand over my head. His hand was cold. All my body felt cold with his touch.

He looked like a different person, not the same man who had served me fish hours back.

• • •

In the morning, light slanted against a corner of the room. The smell of fresh bread rose from the oven. I didn't remember how I'd come back to bed.

The door was left open. I was thirsty, and the clay pot by my bedside was empty. I looked out the window at the landscape of burnt palms.

I opened my suitcase and looked through the books that I'd brought with me. I had ended up bringing *The Book of the Winds* when packing in a rush. I had found the copy in a used bookstore and hadn't read it yet. It read like an encyclopedia of mental illnesses written in a tone shifting from that of an old medical text to a holy book, its pages yellow and disintegrating.

The boy's mother was boiling water in a kettle on an oil stove. She was spreading dough for more bread.

Everybody else was gone.

I asked her where her husband was, but I couldn't fully understand her response. I was hoping that I could ask the father about the night before. I had been so shocked at the time that I'd just watched. I doubted that I'd just dreamed it.

The mother poured me tea. I drank it before I dressed. No one had asked me for the remaining payment for the room. I counted the money and gave it to the mother before I left.

• • •

After the drought, men had moved in groups to work farther south.

Oil rigs, refineries, steel. Lonely men away from their families, staring at screens.

More steel factories and refineries were shutting down, letting people go.

In the industrial towns, strikes every day. Tear gas and batons. Union leaders disappeared.

Emergency rooms flooded with diseases no one had heard of. Doctors sent patients home after failing to prescribe medicine.

The men went back to their villages, back to the times when medicine didn't exist.

People of the wind. I'd heard of them from my grandmother. They healed diseases during their ceremonies. Sometimes even people from the cities would go to them.

The ceremony from last night had unsettled me. An unease remained in me since the father's touch.

• • •

I had travelled south to write about what was happening on the rigs.

Nobody had shown interest in my last essay about the extinction of painted storks, and I had eventually failed to get it published.

"Maybe you need to pitch a piece to editors before you waste so much time on it," Tara had said.

"I wouldn't call it a waste of time," I'd responded. I loved researching and writing about birds.

"In a perfect world, you'd be right. But you need to see the results of what you're doing. Otherwise, it's just torture."

The same year, Tara's parents had helped us buy a house. We no longer had to worry about rent.

Once in a while, I would get a request for copy-editing or a commission to write an essay on behalf of a student. But since the failure of the last essay, I had focused mainly on writing a book about my father.

"I am just tired of watching you go through the same painful exercise again and again," Tara said. She was sitting in front of the TV with a beer in her hand.

Whatever the book about my father was, it wasn't the same exercise. It was the first thing that I had done mainly for myself.

We both became silent, as if the conversation hadn't happened. This had become a routine. The pauses taking over and swallowing words.

Her lips trembled.

I felt guilty. I looked at her eyes, wondering if this was about me not making enough money, but that was an unfair assumption.

I drifted around. I wanted to be present, but I wasn't.

Several months into writing the book about my father, I stopped drinking, thinking things might change if I stopped.

At the beginning, Tara was supportive. But after a while, I got a sense that she didn't really care.

I wondered if she was just waiting for me to fail, to remind me that she had known it all along.

Some days, I thought she was having an affair. I would look at her looking at her phone, smiling. I wouldn't have blamed her if she was.

I knew I would be the guilty one.

I no longer talked to her much about what I was working on, or my father. I didn't have much else to talk about.

My days diminished to the word count in the corner of a screen.

Every day an echo of another.

You had to listen hard to hear anything.

• • •

I drove through a landscape of metal, tall chemical towers, furnace flames flaring to the lead-coloured sky. There were steel pipelines wide enough for trucks to pass through. My eyes followed the pipes branching off, smaller pipes coming together, going somewhere else, scaffolding supporting them.

I passed through a gate where they checked my ID, asked me about my trip. I gave them the signed letter that the Editor had provided. The Editor had told me that everything had been coordinated with the Company before my arrival, but I was still concerned whether they would let me pass. I'd driven such a long distance and it'd be unfortunate to have to turn around. The letter was on the agency's letterhead, but it mentioned that I was a freelance journalist.

Security guards with guns looked on. The air smelled of rotten egg and algae.

I fidgeted in the car, the rest of my documents shaking in my hand. I wondered if they would ask many questions.

"Looking for some excitement?" one of the guards asked, tilting his head to see me from the corner of his glasses.

"Open your trunk," another guard said.

I stepped out of the car and opened the trunk. He didn't even come close to look at it. He kept mumbling something to the other guard.

"You can go now," the first guard said. He stamped the letter and gave it back to me. "You can show this at the port," he added, "but they'll want to see it at the next gate, too."

Metal scraping against metal, the sound of pumps and heavy machinery louder than the wailing wind.

At the next gate, they looked at the letter, provided me with a pair of earplugs and a coupon for my next meal. I was told that I'd have to get a security pass at the refinery office. I would then drive south to the seaport, where a helicopter would take me to the rig.

It was lunchtime, so I parked the car and followed the arrows that directed me to the cafeteria. I watched the workers line up in front of it, their yellow hard hats shining under the hot sun.

I sat there alone at a table with my food, watched the other men eat without talking to each other. Here, there was no sign of the strikes and protests I had heard about from the Editor before my departure. Everything seemed in order, as you'd expect from the Company, a shiny surface hiding the rot underneath.

As a journalist, I tried not to go after topics that the state was sensitive to. My father's history and my mother's continuous discouragement had made me conservative. I was diverging from that path now by taking this assignment.

As I separated the tasteless fish from the watery, red sauce, I remembered that I hadn't called Tara since my departure.

I left the cafeteria to call her, but I got only her voice mail. I checked the time, wondering if she was having lunch with her colleagues or was not responding because she was angry that I hadn't called her sooner.

She complained about how much her colleagues bored her. Yet she sat with them at the same table every day.

"You think I like doing it?" she said. "Only ten percent of what I do every day pleases me. By the way, I don't think I am any different from others. That is life for most people, if they're lucky."

Before that conversation, I had always thought she was interested in her job. She always planned things ahead, even spent some of her time working on weekends. I was shocked that I had seen it so differently. With growing older, she had become more like her parents, more accepting and even wanting the security of a domestic life.

The day before, she had watched me load my luggage into the car, her eyes wet.

I had made her favourite dish before I left, turned off the lights, lit candles. I made her laugh during the dinner.

"This was so good," she said. "You hadn't made it for a long time."

After dinner she touched my cheek with her fingers. I kissed her hand, then we kissed. She put her head on my chest as we sat on the sofa, and we both went to sleep like that.

We woke in a panic at around five in the morning, remembering that I hadn't packed.

I threw my clothes and the books on the nearest shelf into my suitcase. I grabbed the tent and sleeping bag from the garage and put them in the trunk. I dressed quickly. I wanted to leave early in the morning to avoid the rush-hour traffic.

"I'm coming back soon," I said, looking at her by the door, though I wasn't convinced my departure was responsible for her tears.

"Be careful, B," she said.

"I will," I said. "I'll call you tomorrow."

I turned and looked at her again as I drove away. I looked at the house that I had little share in paying for.

The apple orchard she had planted in the front yard.

The wind lifted her hair, gave an impression as if she was floating.

She was still waiting on the porch when I turned onto the main street.

. . .

It didn't take long for the food to turn my stomach. I waited at the office of the refinery for my security pass. All the curtains were drawn. The place smelled like an antique market, a stale smell of rotten wood and rust.

Piles of paper on the desks, folders in the cabinets all around the room. The cabinets covered in dust.

An old man sat in dim light behind his desk. He looked at the papers in front of him for a long time before he finally called my name. His computer monitor was off. He checked my ID and the stamped letter, compared the two against each other. He then turned on the monitor in front of him. A blue light lit his desk and reflected from his glasses. He sighed, then opened a drawer and took out a cardboard card, wrote my name inside a box, and handed it to me.

"I don't know why they sent you here — you don't really need this." He sighed.

I got the card and the letter and passed through the security gates again. One of the guards waved at me as I left the refinery.

As I drove south, the sea started to appear behind the dunes. Small fishing boats floated in the distance. The sky turned dark. I rolled down the windows to smell the sea. After driving for a while, I stopped the car and stepped out to take a look at the ocean. I hadn't been there for many years.

The waves were high. They rolled onto each other. They reminded me of the shape of the dunes. Water and wind against the sand. The wind blew the sand toward the sea.

At a distance, bone-coloured shells piled up and formed a small hill.

A boy walked toward me and showed me a necklace made of shells.

"Are you a pearl hunter?" I asked him.

"My brother was," he said.

He became quiet for a while after. "The wind," he said. "The wind takes them before they can marry their women."

I didn't know what to say.

"I am sorry for your brother," I said. "How much for the necklace?"

I counted the cash in my pocket and gave him what he asked for.

I imagined the necklace against Tara's chest.

Two men were pushing their boat into the stormy sea.

The boy disappeared into the landscape.

•　•　•

In the market, the smell of fish. Fishermen cut the fish with long knives, gutted them in plastic tubs. The eyes stared out from platters filled with ice.

In another part of the market, rows of fish lay on their bellies like fat, dead babies.

I followed two men into a dim hole in the wall where fishermen were drinking, waiting for the storm to finish.

Tiger shrimp fried in big pans. The air was thick and rank.

When the men noticed my entrance, they started whispering. The bartender poured a drink into a copper cup and put it in front of me on the counter.

"What brings you here?" the bartender asked. The middle of his moustache was tobacco stained.

"I'm here for work," I said.

"Everybody leaves here, and you're here for work? There is no work here."

"I am a journalist," I said.

Men raised their heads from their tables.

"I haven't heard that one before," the bartender said. "A journalist, here?"

Some men laughed. One of them lifted his chair, put it down near mine. He sat facing me.

"Excuse him. We're tired. We haven't caught anything for days. The storm is not letting go." He spat the tobacco he was chewing into an empty glass.

"Even when we catch something, there is no one buying," said another man.

They all started laughing again. One of them was laughing more loudly than the others. He didn't stop until his shoulders started to shudder. His laughter turned and he threw a green bottle at the wall.

The other men sitting at the same table held him down.

"Get him out of my bar," the bartender said.

CHAPTER 2

To be allowed onto the helicopter, I had to breathe into a machine. This was after I'd finally arrived at the small airport by the seaport. They took my cellphone and laptop and kept them locked in a box. They'd give them back to me when I returned, they said.

They opened my suitcase, looked through the clothes and books.

"You read a lot," they said.

My suitcase bulged after I crammed the crumpled clothes back into it.

They asked me to take off my socks and shoes.

I'd still not talked to Tara. I hadn't known that I wouldn't be able to take my cellphone and laptop with me. They told me they could arrange for me to send messages from the rig. I hadn't been prepared to give up on communication, but I had come a long way and I decided to go through despite this, as long as there was a way to send messages.

Before boarding, they took four of us into a room with a big screen, three men and a woman. The rest were new hires and had arrived at the airport on a plane. I was the only one who hadn't been hired by the Company. I still had to go through the safety training, though it was not as extensive as the others had taken prior to their arrival.

They showed us videos of workers not wearing hard hats or steel-toed boots, working heavy machinery.

Heads crushed under pipes. Sharp objects in eyes.

A cigarette blew up a rig.

At the end, they showed us a video of the facilities offshore, the dining room with platters of seafood on the tables — oysters, lobsters, stuffed fish.

A gym with a woman in yoga pants running on a treadmill.

After the training session, three more people joined us to board the helicopter.

● ● ●

The sun setting. Quiet sea. The rig looked like a chandelier made of wire. The cranes slanted like seabirds waiting for prey.

After we'd landed, I could still hear the sound of the propeller. I didn't know when the humming of the pumps had replaced the sound of the helicopter. To speak to someone, you had to take out your earplugs and shout. The voices wrestled mid-air until one voice overpowered the other into submission.

It wasn't just all the noise, but the variety of dialects that made communicating difficult.

We were shown to the admission desk. The rest of the people on the helicopter were admitted quickly and guided to their rooms. At last the admission staff issued me a cabin in the housekeeping section, which I'd share with the Assistant Cook. They gave me two sets of blue coveralls, a yellow hard hat, steel-toed boots, an orange safety vest. I was now considered part of the day shift, though I wouldn't benefit from the things the staff had access to, like the gym and other facilities.

For the day workers, dinner was served at 6:30 p.m., breakfast at 5:30 a.m.

I'd missed dinner. I asked the Admission Secretary if I'd be able to have dinner with the night staff.

"I'll look into it," she said. As for my request to meet with one of the managers, she said that would have to wait.

"You aren't their top priority right now," she added. She didn't have the accent that I'd heard in the South. She was tall with short hair that made her ears look important.

"Who else can I interview while I am waiting?" I asked.

She looked at the letter from the Editor again and typed something on her keyboard. "Please don't forget that we did not invite you. I am very busy and I haven't been asked to do anything for you that I haven't already done."

One of the maintenance staff led me through a number of narrow, tunnel-like hallways to my cabin. I was eager to get settled there. The cabin was dim and unventilated and had two bunk beds in it. The beds were the size of a coffin. The top bed would be mine. I didn't know what I'd expected, but I was discouraged with the way the trip had begun.

• • •

For my previous essay, I had talked to ornithologists, bird-watchers, and environmental activists. It had been like being introduced into a secret society. They had been excited to share things with me. The deep network of corruption running underneath the surface of everything. Industries dumping their waste into lakes and creeks. Mobs hunting rare birds for taxidermists and private collectors. Lobbyists and agencies covering things up. They had warned me not to include these in my essay.

I hadn't written about any of it and focused on writing about the storks themselves.

How much could I reveal without getting into trouble? That was the question I had to answer each time, and it was going to be even trickier now. In addition, this time I had to talk to people who clearly weren't interested in talking to me.

I wasn't sure where to start.

I put my suitcase in the cabin, changed into my coveralls, and left the room. The empty hallways were covered with worn-out carpet. A ventilator worked against the smell of fish, burnt fat, and sweat.

I felt a pain behind my eyes, in my temples.

Some of the cabin doors had numbers on them. A sign directed me to the cafeteria where the night workers were eating dinner. I could see into the cafeteria through a glass partition. Night workers in their coveralls. I tried my key card and the sliding glass door to the cafeteria didn't open. Workers continued eating and watching. I tried my key card again. When the door didn't open this time, I walked away.

On the deck, I sat outside in the humid air. The full moon

was low in the sky. It looked as if the huge hook hanging from a crane was stabbing the moon.

I took out the earplugs, listened to the sea, but all I heard was the humming of machines.

The night workers gradually showed up on the deck again. They were directing the drill deep into the sea.

Pipes and pulleys everywhere. Cranes moved up and down. Walkie-talkies crackled. The drill screamed against bedrock, penetrating the earth below us.

I was hungry and horny.

Tara. Her body a distant memory.

Camping with her by the lake. My semen in the water like a snake.

A night in a cabin in the mountains. Drunk on wine. Her long eyelashes. The wooden bed creaking.

I put my hand under her dress.

Her firm buttocks.

"You're not yourself tonight," she said. "You're hurting me."

"I love you."

"I feel like I don't know you anymore."

Good memories brought back bitter ones. Everything tainted.

I wished I could go back to the beginning. I wished I could begin again.

I knew it wasn't possible.

I remembered the early days, when I told her that I couldn't just think about her all day or I would never get any work done.

Even when I tried to read a book, I was so distracted that I couldn't make sense of the words.

I would stare out of the window, waiting for her to come back. The sky would change colour. Trees were filled with blossoms. They waved at me.

A pink light diffused through the curtains when she showed up in the alley, returning from work. My heart would beat fast. I waved at her from the window. She smiled, her face opening. Her big hazel eyes.

I heard her every step coming up the stairs.

In the morning, I begged her to call in sick, to stay in bed. And sometimes she did. We stayed in bed like that, talking, listening to music. We stayed until afternoon, until we were both hungry.

"Do you want to go out?" I asked.

"Yes," she said. But we would end up eating stale bread and cheese, standing by my fridge.

My mind went to strange places after that. For some reason, I remembered my first girlfriend when I was a teenager. I had asked her to go to a movie with me one night. She'd told me she was going to study. Later that night, on the street, I saw her walking with another boy, holding hands. I went back home to my room and shut the door. My mother kept asking what was wrong. I didn't know why I remembered it now.

I tried to remember the girl's face, but I couldn't.

I looked at the cranes. The reflection of the moon rippled on the ocean.

I wanted a drink.

Moving fast, the workers became shadows of themselves. I tried to talk to two of them.

"Busy," they said, holding onto their walkie-talkies, looking up at the drill hammering the bedrock. They walked fast. They didn't make eye contact. A number was written on the front of their yellow hard hats. Their headlights moved through the darkness.

My hard hat didn't have a number on it.

I could detect some familiar words if I listened closely to what was being said on the walkie-talkies.

The light from other rigs flickered in the distance.

• • •

The southerners had had worse jobs than working on the rigs for years. They had worked as divers and fishermen. The sea captains hired fishermen who didn't have boats, fishermen who couldn't survive on their own, and used them for pearl hunting.

Long trips out to the middle of the sea. The men would sleep on deck and dive as the sun rose. They'd dive with a rope attached to them, a basket on their backs. When they returned breathless, the sea captain would whip them with a wet branch and make them go down again.

Sometimes their dead bodies returned to the deck with an empty basket.

The living ones came back broken from the sea, afraid of trees, afraid of shadows. They would escape, roam the dilapidated castles like birds trapped in the desert.

If they had a family, they might call for the people of the wind. Make a sacrifice. Make a play ceremony, tame their winds.

• • •

Back in the cabin, the Assistant Cook rolled over on his bed.

The cabin was dark. I could see only his silhouette. I found my way through the cabin and climbed onto the top bunk. I took off my boots and removed the earplugs. Even in the cabin, you could hear the noise.

"Go to sleep soon or you'll miss tomorrow's breakfast, too."
He rubbed his eyes. "I left something for you on your bed. I
saw you couldn't get into the cafeteria."

On my bed, there was a piece of bread, two dates, a bottle
of water.

I gulped down half of the water, then swallowed the bread
and chewed the meaty dates. "Thank you!" I said with my
mouth full. I took a sleeping pill and drank the rest of the
water. I didn't have that many of the pills.

The ceiling was only inches away from my face.

After less than a day, I was having more doubts about accepting the assignment.

"Better go to sleep," the Assistant Cook said. Soon, he started snoring.

The room wasn't ventilated, and the Assistant Cook's
breathing sounded laboured.

I undressed and closed my eyes. I moved the pillow around
and pulled the sheets over my legs.

The sheets felt damp.

• • •

In the morning, the Assistant Cook woke me for breakfast. Apparently, he'd called me several times and I hadn't
heard him. He was standing on the ladder and was shaking
me.

I followed him through the hallways to the cafeteria, still
disoriented. Workers lined up to fill their steel plates. They sat
in tables of four, left their hard hats on the tables. The Assistant
Cook shook hands with some of them. They eyed me briefly
and carried their plates to their tables.

The coffee tasted burnt. I could drink it only after adding cream. I filled my plate with fruits, a boiled egg, a piece of buttered toast.

It was my first proper meal for several days. I couldn't understand most of the exchanges between the men sitting at our table. Out of politeness, the Assistant Cook turned toward me once in a while and asked me a question, interpreted something others had said.

"Where do you come from?"

"Which agency do you work for?"

When I said I was a freelancer, they looked down into their plates in disappointment and sipped their tea.

I heard the Assistant Cook say the Editor's name. One of the men nodded. They had probably heard the Editor's name before. I hadn't told the Assistant Cook anything about my assignment, so I was a little shaken by this exchange. Then I remembered that I had left the letter from the agency on my suitcase, and he'd probably just seen it.

I got a sense they knew that my mission was going to be related to the rig workers.

At first I'd been shocked that the Editor had reached out to me for the report. I wasn't known as a journalist and had little experience with this type of fieldwork. I had taken the assignment partially because of the Editor's reputation, though the Editor's current position with the agency seemed unstable. Despite everything, he'd offered a good advance, which I'd thought would please Tara. But I couldn't fully understand why they hadn't assigned someone from the agency for this.

I watched the workers wipe their plates clean with bread. Drink water. They kept asking for more water.

One of them said something that I didn't understand, and they all laughed.

I stared at the TV, pretending I was watching what was on.

After breakfast I followed the Assistant Cook to the deck to watch the unloading of the c-cans. I wasn't sure who else to talk to. I was hoping that I'd slowly find more leads to direct me to something.

My hard hat sat crooked on my head and kept falling off until the Assistant Cook stopped me and showed me how it should be fitted.

The cargo ship had arrived close to the platform. The sky was the colour of concrete. The high waves moved the ship up and down.

The platform was anchored at sixteen points and wobbled with the waves.

The Crane Operator tied the c-cans to the crane with steel chains. The Assistant Cook guided the Operator with his hand, moving his hand up and down or drawing a circle, but the c-cans kept landing on top of each other. The Operator swore at the wind and swore at the sea.

The Assistant Cook ignored him. This made the Crane Operator even angrier.

The Assistant Cook was a tall man with bad posture and a birthmark the size of a tennis ball on his neck. The night before, I had listened to him snoring and talking in his sleep, making sounds that resembled words from some forgotten language.

I'd eventually gone to sleep to the sound of his breathing.

I stood there and watched until all the c-cans were on deck.

The Operator dozed as the Assistant Cook untied the chains and opened the c-cans, unloading what was inside onto carts. Inside the c-cans, there were boxes of mangoes and bananas. Ramen noodles and rice. Rolls of paper towel. Frozen fish. Containers of water.

"Why do you have to unload everything on your own? Shouldn't someone from maintenance help you?" I asked.

"It's my job," he said.

"How long have you been working here?"

"Twenty years," he said. "I do what I am asked to."

"But you do have a union?" I asked.

"Right," he said.

I wasn't sure if his tone was sarcastic or secretive. He'd been pretty nice to me, but he seemed a bit annoyed now. I was about to ask him more questions, but I didn't want to move too quickly. I thought it'd be best to wait for a better occasion.

I still wanted to say something to continue the conversation, but I couldn't find anything else to say. For a journalist, I was terrible at making small talk.

He searched around for a forklift and couldn't find it. We found a wheelbarrow instead, opened the packages, and loaded things into it. I pushed the wheelbarrow full of food, following the Assistant Cook toward the kitchen.

A group of technicians came by the cargo ship and asked the Operator to unload another group of c-cans full of pipes and machine parts.

"Fuck," the Assistant Cook said. "Now all of them are busy with other stuff. It's always like this, and the kitchen gets blamed for lack of food variety."

When we got to the kitchen, the Assistant Cook asked me to leave everything behind the door.

"I'll take care of the rest. It's not going to work like this. I'll have to find a better way."

By the door, a technician was welding a big flange to a pipe. He was wearing a face shield.

"Look away," the Assistant Cook said.

When the work was done, the Assistant Cook showed me the welds. "Look at it, it's a work of art."

I didn't know much about welding, but I nodded.

"Thanks for your help today," he said.

"Thanks for showing me around," I responded.

• • •

People were thirsty in the South. The land was dry. Some villages didn't have any water to drink. They would try to buy drinking water from other villages if they had money. Well water got trucked for kilometres. Sometimes they didn't have enough money and begged for a sip of water for their children from the ships that passed by. The sea was all they had to live on. They survived on the fish they caught, the dates from the few palm trees they owned. Jobs on oil rigs had been a way out of this misery until a couple of years ago, but now things were worse again.

The oil production was greater than the demand for it.

The fishing had become harder. Small fishing boats didn't stand a chance against big industrial ships.

More people were back in the deserted villages, trying to work the palm yards. The wind howled through the dilapidated clay houses, the water level low in the wells.

The locals believed bad spirits travelled with the wind. They were more likely to find the poor and the weak. Bad spirits waited around dried wells, shallow creeks, and under the sea.

• • •

The Admission Secretary told me that they wouldn't be able to give me a new computer, but they could print my emails for me. There was an old laptop that worked only as a word processor. I could use it for typing my messages, and the messages could be transferred through a memory stick to the Secretary's computer, sent to whomever I wanted.

"This was the best arrangement we could come up with given the security risks," the Secretary said. "It's additional work I didn't sign up for, but we were told to do it, so we'll do it."

I didn't know who "we" referred to. Whoever it was, this meant they could read my emails to the Editor and to Tara. I would have to limit any important interactions through this channel. This wasn't what I'd expected when, at the seaport, they'd told me I'd be able to send messages.

I still hadn't met any of the rig managers. That morning, as we were walking to the cafeteria, the Assistant Cook had pointed at the conference room where the managers were having their daily meeting.

"Their rooms have an ocean view and only one bed in them," he said. "That's the main difference."

"And do they have air conditioning in their rooms?"

"Sure."

I wondered if that was all that separated them from the others.

I got the laptop and sat on the other side of the Secretary's counter to type a message to Tara. A worker in blue coveralls came and dropped off a piece of paper. They whispered something, and the Secretary giggled. I couldn't see the Secretary's face from where I was sitting. The worker's big hands were hidden behind the counter. They continued whispering. I couldn't hear what they said. I looked at the guy's badge and noticed that it had only a number written on it.

The laptop made a loud noise and took a long time to turn on. The Company's logo appeared on the screen. I opened the word processor and typed:

> *It was a long way, but I got here safely. I hope I didn't worry you by not contacting you sooner. I tried to call you but only got your voice mail. They didn't let me bring my cellphone and laptop here. It would be best not to discuss private and personal matters through email.*

But the last sentence made the tone paranoid and unfriendly. I deleted it and added:

> *Let me know how you are. I've missed you very much.*

> *B.*

When I lifted my head, the man was no longer there. The Secretary gave me a form to fill out, a memory stick to copy the file onto. She told me that the file would be sent out right away.

As soon as I left the reception area, I regretted not sending a more intimate message. Tara was going to find the tone cold. I'd panicked about the Company staff reading my emails, but what was worse?

I remembered the first letter my father had sent us. I didn't know why I remembered this. With his letter, he'd sent me a remote-control toy car. The customs office had broken an electrical chip off the car. I cried so much that my mother took me searching all over the city for a repair shop that could fix it. Everybody dismissed us. When we went back home, my mother went to the bedroom and pressed her face into the pillow, then shut the door to their bedroom.

The sun was setting.

Sunsets often take me back to that day.

I didn't know if my mother knew then that my father wasn't coming back.

· · ·

I got lost on my way back to the cabin. I bumped into two technicians servicing a pump.

"Clogged," one of them said.

They closed two big valves to isolate the pump, turned on the spare. The second man started torquing a wrench with a long handle.

They timed everything and took notes in a logbook.

When they opened up and dismantled the pump, they looked on in disbelief.

I couldn't see what they saw from where I was standing.

"What is this?" the guy with the wrench asked.

"Shit … shit," the other man repeated.

· · ·

Back in my cabin, there were two yellow envelopes on the floor. One of them was thicker than the other.

I opened the thinner envelope. The letter was from the Editor.

> *Is everything going all right? How is the report coming together? Would be great if you can send me what you've got so far. We can take it one step at a time.*

I didn't have anything written yet. I didn't have any interviews lined up. I was surprised that he was expecting an update from me so soon.

I opened the laptop and typed:

> *I am working on the report as I am settling in. I was not permitted to bring my own laptop and have to send everything through the rig staff. I'd like to minimize any security risks. I will submit my report upon departure from the rig.*

> *B.*

I reread my message, then crossed out the sentence before last. I didn't want to attract unnecessary attention. I assumed that the Editor would understand why I didn't want to send him anything through this channel.

It was becoming more evident that I hadn't asked enough questions before my trip. I hadn't known what I was getting into, or what the Editor's expectations were. I had been excited about the prospect of publishing the book about my father, about this paid mission that followed right after it. I realized that I had skipped some important steps and rushed into accepting the assignment.

I left the cabin. Through the long hallways of the rig, the walls became like tall trees in the woods. The numbers on the doors blurred like patches of leaves when you're running from someone following you.

I sped up my steps.

I gave the memory stick to the Secretary. In return, she handed me a piece of paper. She looked at me like a police officer would at a driver slurring his words.

I assumed she'd read the letter before me.

"It just arrived. I didn't get a chance to put it in an envelope yet," she said.

> *I was worried. You've been gone a week without any messages. Why didn't you call me before you got there?*
>
> *T.*

I had told her that I'd called her, but she'd dismissed that.

"Just to make things easier for both parties," the Secretary said, "compile all of your messages to send them only once a day. As you can see, I am very busy."

I hurried back to my cabin. The cleaner had her cart in the hallway. She was standing in a cabin with the door open. She was a bit plump and had thick, curly hair. When she saw me passing, she stepped out of the cabin. Her thin eyebrows looked like inverted Vs.

"You don't have to work now?" she asked. She was probably in her late forties.

"I don't work for the rig."

"Oh, good for you."

"You don't like working here?"

"It's fine. It pays the bills, and I don't have to talk to anyone for weeks."

"Isn't it hard?"

"I like missing home and missing my husband. It's good to know that somebody is expecting me somewhere."

"I can relate to that," I said. Though I wasn't that sure Tara would be expecting me.

"But he complains that I don't call him enough from here. He is upset every time until I go home, then things go back to normal until I leave again."

It had become harder to call the longer I hadn't called Tara. I wouldn't know what to talk about if I was able to call now. I didn't know how to explain that in my letter.

It never worked when you felt guilty and tried to explain yourself. It always made everything worse.

But the longer I didn't tell her things, the harder it was to explain them.

I used to tell her everything before, before I had found myself alone with petty secrets.

Unlike me, the staff had tokens they could use to make calls from a satellite phone.

"Why don't you call him more often, then?" I asked her.

"I get used to not talking. I need to regain momentum to break the silence."

I understood what she meant, yet she didn't have trouble speaking to me.

"To be honest, even when I go back, I don't feel like being with anyone for a little while," she said.

"Would you mind skipping my room today? I have work to do that requires focus."

"Skip," she repeated with a pause. Her pronunciation of the word sounded peculiar. Her face changed as if she was tasting something unexpected. Had I offended her?

She sprayed a rag with disinfectant and started cleaning a cabin door. When I said goodbye, she didn't respond.

In the cabin, I climbed into my bed with the laptop and the second envelope. I propped the pillow between the wall and my back. I wanted to respond to Tara, not let things become worse between us again.

I opened the laptop and typed a couple of sentences. But I was getting anxious about the thicker envelope. I kept wondering what was inside it. I couldn't postpone opening it.

The envelope wasn't something I was expecting. The email was from my publisher and included the edits on the first chapter of my book.

He'd printed the manuscript, commented on it, then scanned the commented version. The Secretary had printed the emailed document in colour.

Many lines were crossed out with red pen, the Publisher's handwriting all over the text.

I started looking at his comments.

Anything about my father being laid off from the factory had been removed from the chapter.

Excerpts of the interviews I had conducted with his former colleagues and friends were all cut out. I had included many of these colleagues as anonymous interviewees, as I was concerned about their safety. I wondered if that had something to do with the Publisher's reaction.

What remained from the first chapter were mainly photos that I had included, along with the text the Publisher had written.

A photo of my father in his store after he was laid off.

A photo of him with his own father when he was ten, on a boat on a lake.

A copy of the newspaper showing my father's name as the winner of a student poetry prize.

A photo of the remote-control car he had sent me with his last letter. I had kept the broken car all these years.

The Publisher had added descriptions in the margins and asked me to expand more in some places, including about my father's childhood, his parents, and his education in high school.

The words blurred into each other. My breath became the breath of a pearl hunter opening an empty shell.

> *Please implement my edits to this chapter. We need to get this ready soon, but it will need some restructuring. Unfortunately, it still requires lots of work.*

This was written in the body of the email. He'd read the whole manuscript before. Had said he'd loved it, then.

Something had changed.

Heat rushed into my head. His prose rang like the noise of an air compressor.

I was furious. The book wasn't supposed to be a biography of my father.

It was my attempt to find out who he was, to understand why he'd left and stopped communicating with us.

The Publisher wanted a different manuscript now.

I thought it would be best not to respond. I needed to talk to him in person. I could stand behind my choices, explain why things were as they were.

I went to bed, covered my head with the blanket. I wanted to sleep and wake up to a different reality.

I blinked in the darkness. I heard the rustling of my body against the sheets, the humming of the ventilators in the hallway.

I smelled my own sweat.

Unfortunately, I was awake.

The walls were thin as paper. Once in a while I heard people speaking or shouting in the hallway, but couldn't make out their words.

I was used to rejection, but this felt different.

The promise of publication had given me hope. It had helped me stay sober.

But it had been a mirage.

The bed smelled like a bed in a train.

I rolled over and lay on my side. I removed the blanket and looked at the black boot marks left on the grey wall, the greasy fingerprints along the cracks, insects smeared on the wall.

I ran my fingers over the cracks.

I wondered if I was partially to blame, for believing people for things they said.

I took another sleeping pill.

• • •

I woke up to a man leaning over me in my bed. The lights were off. Like a dream when you wake up to a stranger in your room, I wanted to scream.

I didn't know where I was.

Then I noticed the birthmark. I remembered the morning and the c-cans.

"You scared me," I said.

"I thought you'd miss dinner again," the Assistant Cook said. "You missed lunch."

His hand rested on my shoulder like it was trying to tell me something.

"Is everything all right?" he asked. "You disappeared without saying anything. Have you been sleeping ever since?"

My mouth had a taste to it. My tongue felt heavy. I was distracted by the birthmark.

"I am okay," I said.

"Were you having a dream?" he asked. "You shouldn't stay alone here so much."

In my dream, I had been swimming in a creek, following a painted stork. It led me to a marsh where the corpses of other storks floated on the water through the reeds and canes. I found one of the bodies that was still moving, tried to hold it and swim back to the creek.

The reeds tangled with my shins. I was sinking in the marsh. The water was black like oil. Viscous like tar.

"Things haven't been exactly easy," I said. "I am going through a rough patch."

He moved his head around like he was looking for something in the cabin. A worn-out towel hung from a hook on the wall. His eyes stopped there.

The cabin smelled like a hospital room. Of sickness when you don't leave your bed for days. I looked at the other corner of the room where my suitcase was.

"Let's get you out of this cabin," he said.

"I need to change," I said.

"It'll help to freshen up," he said.

I found my toothbrush in the suitcase and took it along with me.

In the hallway, the fluorescent lamps fused into each other, became a long block of light as I walked faster. I wondered for how many days I had been on the rig, how many days I hadn't showered.

In the bathroom, one of the toilets had overflowed, a stream of waste on the floor. Flies flapped their wings onto the lamps.

I held my breath. I tiptoed around the puddle, splashed water on my face. I looked at the mirror, then brushed my teeth until my gums bled. I spat red into the sink. I gargled several times until the water was clear.

If Tara were here, she would make me shave. Every day, before sitting at my desk, I'd wake up and shave and shower as if I were actually going to work.

"You need a better routine to function," she'd said.

I ran my fingers through my beard. I remembered that I still hadn't answered her email.

I took off my shirt and splashed water under my armpits.

When the Assistant Cook knocked at the bathroom door, I put my shirt back on and buttoned the top of my coveralls.

I looked at the mirror again. I still wasn't used to my new appearance: a man with a beard in blue coveralls. My hard hat had gone crooked again, but I didn't try to straighten it.

"Let's go," I said.

• • •

At dinner, the Assistant Cook sat with me. My scrawny figure differentiated me from the rest of the crowd.

Workers waved at the Assistant Cook as they passed our table. He was friends with so many workers, but he was still sitting with me.

I wondered if it was just out of pity that he was doing this.

I remembered my high school days. Going to the bathroom to eat my snacks there, alone, to not be in the cafeteria, to not have to talk to others. The walls and doors engraved with sexual drawings and brown stains. I got used to eating things cold, with the terrible smell in the background. Once I heard a boy force another one to blow him in the next stall as I was eating an apple.

I couldn't eat much. The sight and the smell of fish made me queasy. I pictured the father's hand removing the fish scales with his machete.

"I don't feel well," I said.

"Do you want something else?" the Assistant Cook asked. "Have some bread, at least."

The cafeteria was very cold, or I was getting sick.

"You look pale," the Assistant Cook said.

He was probably at least ten years older than me. How comfortable he seemed in everything he did.

I watched the others, laughing, talking. They all moved around with such ease.

For a moment, I wondered if they were all okay on the rig, if my being here was some kind of a joke. That I was going through this for nothing.

I felt something like a rope twisting in my stomach. Sweat beaded on my forehead.

"Do you have kids?" I asked the Assistant Cook. I didn't know why I asked him this.

"Yes, two daughters and a son," he said. "And you — don't say it! Let me guess. I think probably a daughter."

I told him that we didn't have any children.

His smile wilted. He paused. I thought the news had disappointed him.

"Sometimes you keep going just for them. It's a strange thing." He sighed.

I remembered my father before he disappeared. The more years passed, the more my memories of him faded. They lost their colour and texture. Their gap like a missing tooth. You kept running your tongue over what wasn't there anymore.

When I was in fourth grade, we were supposed to make these electrical circuits for our science course. My father was long gone by then. We'd accepted that he wasn't coming back. A number of lamps and an alarm switch would turn on, but they had to all work with the same battery. I had built a simple circuit with a single lamp. My mother helped me with wiring and setting it up on a wood panel. She had no experience with something like that, yet she always tried her best. My lamp turned on for only a few seconds, then flickered and died. It was too late to build another one.

Next day at school, my classmates showed up with complicated circuits on big panels, some so big their parents had to bring them in their cars. I sat in my seat and watched everyone else. The teacher tested the circuits one by one.

They were all excited about their circuits.

I thought about the remote-control car again, about the chip that was missing.

Something that had always been missing.

I wasn't even sure that it was something to do with my father.

• • •

After dinner the Assistant Cook took me to the control room.

"We need to cheer you up," he said.

Big men were dozing off in front of screens. Empty bottles of Coke and greasy paper food bags were on the desks. The room smelled of feet.

"Can we be here without permission?"

"Don't worry," he said. "I got your back."

Numbers showing flow and pressure fluctuated on the screens. Pumps and valves turned on and off, going from blue to red and back.

You could click on the screen, watch their trends, watch what the equipment was doing at that moment.

I was feeling better after leaving the cafeteria.

Oil and gas separated in pressurized vessels, flowed to the shore to refineries and petrochemical plants.

Every day, more refineries were shutting down. More rigs were being abandoned. Oil tankers floated on foreign seas without any destination.

One of the screens started flashing and beeping. An operator woke and looked at the screen. He typed something on his keyboard. At first a page with a card game opened on his screen.

On another tab, a woman with big breasts was inserting a light bulb into her vagina.

"Imagine that thing breaking there." The Assistant Cook laughed.

The operator looked our way, then ignored us and closed his eyes again. The beeping stopped. The operator's walkie-talkie barked. The voice coming through wasn't clear.

The Assistant Cook took out a small camera from his pocket.

"Can you have a camera here?" I asked. At the safety training, we had been told that no video recording was permitted. They'd let me bring my voice recorder, though.

The Assistant Cook pointed the camera at me when I asked him this.

I wasn't even sure if I was permitted to be there. "What are you doing?" I asked. I hid my face with my hands.

"It isn't even recording." He laughed.

He put the camera back in his pocket and pulled me outside the control room.

"I like to know what is going on," he said. "People don't know anything about what is going on around them."

He took me to another room with a big screen. All the workers were shown as numbers on the rig map.

"But how do they track us?"

"Your key card," he said.

"So, wouldn't they see where we are now?" I asked. "How do you even have access to all these rooms?"

"I have my ways, and I've reached a point that I don't care. My children are grown now, so I am not as worried as I was before."

I tried to count the dots on the map, but couldn't follow them all. The points kept moving around on the screen. I had trouble knowing exactly where to look.

"So, you don't fear being fired anymore?" I asked.

"Let them fire me. They've already demoted me. I was initially hired as an electrical engineer. Worked eighteen years as one. I was hired when oil was first discovered around here. It was even before the drought. I was never afraid of them. But I had to feed my kids and send them to school. So, I kept my mouth shut. I know all the control systems in all the rigs. But I like working in the kitchen. Less of the stupid politics. I do everything, yet my title is Assistant Cook." He sighed. "There is something else that I haven't told anyone. I assume they know it, so they don't bother with me much."

I looked into his eyes. There were black clouds underneath them. I wondered if they had been there before, and I was only noticing them now.

He looked at the floor. "I have cancer. Actually, two different types of cancer."

I didn't know how to react. I was moved by the news and that he'd told me about it.

"I am so sorry," I said. I felt sorry for my earlier thoughts, for not having seen this at all.

"That's cool," he said. "Maybe you'll write my life story some day?" He laughed, trying to change the mood.

●　●　●

Outside on the deck, the smell of rotten eggs. Roughnecks in yellow ponchos. The flame from the flare gas pointed down. The rain slammed onto the cranes and washed the dark shadows into the sea.

"I want to go back to the cabin," I said.

"It's too early for that. We need to have some fun."

The Assistant Cook guided me under a corrugated roof behind the kitchen. We were already wet.

Piled-up garbage bags. Rain washing through cigarette butts on the deck. He lit a cigarette and offered me one.

I asked if smoking here wasn't dangerous.

"No one cares," he responded.

I didn't say no, though I hadn't smoked in years. I inhaled the smoke and coughed.

A girl in coveralls walked out of the kitchen back door. She was struggling to maintain her balance. Mascara had washed down around her eyes, making black rivulets on her sharp cheeks. She had brown eyes and a piercing in her nose. A ponytail poked out from under her hard hat. She was muscular with broad shoulders.

"Is she drunk?" I asked the Assistant Cook.

"I'm not drunk," she said, hearing me. She held her lighter high in the air, looking at it as if it was some mysterious object.

"Can you fix this, baby?" she asked me. She brought the lighter down and looked at it again.

I took the lighter from her, dried it on a part of my coveralls that wasn't wet. I shook it several times until I got it to work.

When she saw this, she put her hands behind my neck, rose on her toes and brought her face close to mine.

"Thank you," she said, looking into my eyes. Our hard hats bumped. The rain drummed on corrugated metal. My cigarette fell from my hand. The red glow hissed in water.

She didn't taste of alcohol, but of something peppermint.

She stepped back, staggered away, but not before kissing the Assistant Cook on the cheek.

"He is my reliable person." She pointed at the Cook. "The only person I trust here."

"Time for bed," she said and walked back through the door.

"She likes you," the Assistant Cook said.

"I'm married," I said, the wetness from her hands on the back of my neck. "She was just drunk!" The taste of peppermint remained in my mouth. I tongued the tip of my front teeth. The hair on the back of my neck prickled.

"Can they get alcohol here?" I asked, pretending nothing had happened.

"They can get everything." He laughed. "What do you need?"

"Nothing," I said. "All I want is to understand what is going on here."

"We've made wine in the kitchen, but getting pills is easier. There's all kinds of stuff. The nurse makes good money off it."

I thought about the woman I had followed in the city.

I had been driving around after my writing hadn't gone anywhere, ending up at the bookstore. I'd started drinking before leaving the house and had taken my flask with me for the road.

A tall figure dressed in black. Black eyes. Black wavy hair. Headphones in her ears.

She was flipping through the pages of a novel I liked. After she noticed me, she smiled, then went to the cash register, paid for the book.

I was tempted to go talk to her, but I couldn't.

I watched her walk out of the store. She turned and looked at me again as I was getting into my car.

The lights of the cars were colourful dots on my foggy windshield. I drove slowly. I didn't know why I started following her.

She knew she was being followed, but she didn't stop. Finally, she got to her apartment, took her keys out of her bag, opened the door.

I parked the car several metres away. I was ready to go home, to get into bed beside Tara. She would pretend she was asleep, pull the blanket over her, roll to the other edge of the bed. Or complain that I reeked of alcohol. But the woman left the door open and walked in my direction. At first I thought she was going to ask me to leave, threaten to call the police. I was embarrassing myself.

But she asked if I wanted to go in and grabbed my hand, smiling. I noticed she was slightly taller than me. She had a small mouth and lips that had an unusual colour to them. When she smiled, I could see her gums.

I wanted to drive away, but ended up following her into the building instead.

She had a big apartment with high ceilings and white walls. In the living room, patterned ceramic plates were installed on a wall. The furniture was light grey.

I was a little surprised that she didn't have any books. I wondered if they were in another room.

The apartment had a clinical feel, like nobody lived in it, but I didn't question this.

She mixed us drinks in a shaker without asking me what I wanted. I wanted to start a conversation, but she came closer, unbuttoned my shirt, put her hand on my chest.

"Your heart is beating so fast." She smiled, then asked me to undress and shower first.

I remembered the light blue tiles in the bathroom, patches of her skin, the fuzzy hair on the back of her neck. Her small mouth taking me in. A tie of her hair in my hand.

She moved from her knees to her stomach.

The wrinkled white sheets had a yellow tint. They had her smell. The whole bedroom smelled of her.

I started crying as I was holding her, her black eyes staring at me.

A dull light emanated from a lamp on the bedside table.

I didn't remember anything else. When I left her apartment and went back home. If Tara said anything.

In the morning, I woke up on the sofa in our living room. I was thirsty. My head hurt. The car wasn't in the garage but parked in the alley.

A couple of weeks later, I felt a burning when I tried to pee. I drove around for hours trying to find her apartment.

All the apartments looked alike: grey blocks of concrete with tiny balconies. Through the windows, TV lights flickered in dark rooms. Silhouettes had dinner in silence. Trees had no leaves. A drunken man limped home to his children.

I didn't know what to tell Tara.

In the doctor's office, I urinated into a small cup. I had to leave and drink more water, wait, come back, and urinate again.

In the examination room, I undressed and covered myself with a paper sheet the doctor had pointed to. I was like a cheaply wrapped gift.

The paper rustled as the doctor studied the skin around my penis. I was shivering.

"Do you sleep with men or women?" she asked.

I waited for the results. I was anxious as to what to do next.

I wanted to disappear.

I wondered if my father might have disappeared because of shame, if shame was stronger than fear.

But there was no sign of disease when the results came back. The burning gradually went away.

Anytime I went to the bookstore after, I looked around, thinking I might run into the woman.

I told myself that what had happened didn't mean much, that it'd just happened once.

I'd done it only because I was drunk. But what had she seen in me?

Maybe there was something more to it.

I thought of how I had cried as I'd held her.

I wanted to tell Tara about it. But I was afraid that she would think even less of me.

Though no one could think less of me than I did myself, then.

A pretentious parasite. A pervert.

I was nervous that I didn't remember all the details of the night.

The woman had disappeared into thin air.

I couldn't go on like that.

I told myself that things would get better if I stopped drinking.

•   •   •

The fat executive had *ACCOUNTABILITY* printed on a large piece of paper taped to his office door. You could hear his heavy breathing from a distance, the floors shaking as he moved around the rig. With his tall, muscular assistant following him, the two of them looked more like mobsters.

"Everybody is afraid of him, but he is the lowest-ranked one, and probably the only one who may talk to you," the Assistant Cook said. "He does most of the groundwork for them."

"The Secretary told me the managers won't have time to talk to me."

"The other two executives only come here for meetings with the fat man and don't interact with anybody else. Their doors are always locked," he said. "I am not sure how much value you can get out of talking to any of them. Even if they talk to you, they're not going to tell you anything you want to hear."

Usually, I would develop a list of people I wanted to interview. I learned about them and their backgrounds in advance. In this case, I didn't know how I could do that.

I wasn't even sure if it was less risky to talk to managers or workers.

I waited behind the fat man's door for less than a minute, listening. There weren't any guards around. I had prepared some questions to ask in case I could convince him to talk. I knocked and opened the door without waiting for his response.

"What do you need?" the fat man asked, not raising his eyes from the documents in front of him on his desk.

"I'm here to —"

"I know who you are and what you're here to do," he said. "Look, we're busy professionals here and don't have time for games. If you want to stick around and treat this as a trip with free food and lodging, you're welcome to do so. I hope this was communicated clearly to you upon your arrival. If not, consider this your last notice. Your intentions may be genuine or naive. But if you start wasting our time, I'll have to act. They've been reviewing what you're doing and it doesn't seem very constructive."

He pointed at a chess board in the corner of his office.

"Remember this! I am always at least five steps ahead of others. There's a reason that everything runs like clockwork here."

Obviously, that wasn't the case, but there was no point in me arguing about that. I was trying to come up with something to say.

"Close the door behind you." He made a fist of his right hand and hit the desk. His tea glass fell from the edge of the desk and shattered into pieces.

He went back to signing the documents in front of him.

The Assistant Cook had been right. There was no point in trying to talk to him.

•   •   •

"The guards here aren't armed, as far as I know — at least yet," the Assistant Cook said. "I don't know about elsewhere."

I had yet to see one of the guards.

"This is bigger than just this rig," he said. "Maybe even bigger than the Company."

I recorded the Assistant Cook on my recorder, scribbled additional notes in my notebook. Being around him made me less timid.

"Have there been any strikes on this particular rig?"

"No. But the pay was delayed. There were suicides. One of the workers hanged himself from his bunk bed. The cleaning lady found his body in the cabin. Another cut his wrist in the shower. Some union members have disappeared after."

We were sitting side by side on his bed. He'd stayed awake to answer my questions.

"Many workers take pills. I'm sure the management knows about this. They used to be very strict about such things, but now they're only concerned about the strikes. Who knows — maybe they even take a cut on the sales of the drugs."

He was yawning when he finished speaking. He had become quiet, talking with his eyes closed.

"They try to balance things out. In the end, what matters to them most is to maintain their production rate. But now there is less demand. So, who knows what they think."

I moved over to my own bed and turned off the recorder. I still wanted to talk to other workers on the rig, though that wasn't going to be easy. Maybe he could help me with that.

"I know worse things have happened on other rigs," the Assistant Cook said after a pause.

"Like what?"

"Sorry — I cannot say more."

"But you can't just make a remark and leave it like that," I said. "Do you at least know who is leading the union activities on site? Is there somebody local that I can talk to?"

"There are so many risks," he said. "I've trusted you so far, hoping that you'd help the workers. But even if I knew, I couldn't tell you this. You have to understand that I know the limits better than you do. You better trust me. Even this may not be tolerated. You may or may not be safe in your home in the city after this.

"But be sure: they'll come after the informants," he said. "The union now acts as one body. The representatives are not revealed. The negotiators only take messages between the management and the union. They have no power to negotiate on the union's behalf."

I understood his concern. He'd already helped me so much. If I had been sure I could help them, I would have pushed him more.

I trusted him and I didn't want to put anybody at risk.

After that conversation, I feared the consequences of my mission less, though some of his remarks should've had the opposite effect. There was something about him or his demeanour that put me at ease.

Suddenly, everything seemed clearer. Like after I had been sober for several months.

I climbed down and put the recorder back into my suitcase. The Assistant Cook's eyes were still closed. His chest was heaving. I picked up the laptop and went back to my bunk with it.

On the laptop, I typed a letter to Tara to send out the next morning.

> *Sorry for not contacting you from the road earlier. I tried and got your voice mail. The coverage wasn't so good after. Things have been weird so far. The staff are very hostile, except for my roommate, who has helped me a lot.*
>
> *By the way, I got a letter from my publisher yesterday, asking for major changes to the manuscript, but his comments don't make much sense to me. I am shocked by the change in his attitude. I guess I'll have to talk to him when I am back.*

*But things are gradually improving with my
work here. At least, I have a better plan for the
report now.*

I read it again and wondered if it would cause concern if the
Company read the message, and I decided that I didn't care.

"I've lost everything," the Assistant Cook said as I was typing. "I've got nothing else to lose."

"Why do you say that?" I said. "Don't say that."

I looked down from my bed. He was snoring.

Had he said that sentence in his sleep? Or had I imagined
hearing it? What I'd heard was contrary to what I knew of him.

• • •

In my dream, I was in the tall woman's building again. I was
afraid somebody would recognize me. Water dripped from the
ceiling into pails. Plaster fell off the walls. The sound of the
dripping echoed in the hallway.

The elevator door was corroded with rust. As I looked
around, I decided that going to her place had been a mistake.
I got back onto the elevator. As I was going down, I changed
my mind again, stopped the elevator. This time, I took the
stairs up to her apartment. The door of her unit was open. Her
apartment was empty. All the furniture was gone.

This is for the best, I thought. It was over, then. Time would
wash it away. I was about to leave when the door behind me
opened.

She was standing there naked. She wrapped a soft blanket
around me and pulled me inside toward her. I felt the warmth
of her skin.

The apartment didn't look familiar. I didn't know if this was the same woman or not.

I woke with a hard-on. The Assistant Cook had left the cabin. He'd left the light on. I checked the time and realized that I had missed breakfast again.

I packed a towel, clean underwear, and coveralls inside a plastic bag and went to the bathroom. The shower curtains were transparent. I went into one of the stalls and turned on the tap. The water was warm. I looked around before stroking my penis.

I pictured the woman in the dream, the tall woman from the bookstore in bed with me. I pulled at my pubic hair like she had. The steam rose in the stall.

A pressure in my chest. A vacuum in my thighs.

I washed myself with soap afterward.

After I dressed, I went back to the cabin and saved the email from the night before onto the memory stick. I walked to the front desk to send the email to Tara.

The Secretary wasn't in her coveralls anymore. She was wearing a black tank top.

I had received a letter from Tara.

> *What the fuck, B? You just say something and disappear AGAIN?*
>
> *T.*

I didn't change what I'd written, pretending that I hadn't seen the last message. After sending the message, I went back to the cabin and continued working on the report in my bunk. I listened to the recording. I tried to make a narrative out of what I had observed so far. I was distracted and sleepy. My left eye kept twitching. I pressed my thumb on my eyelid and held it there.

A high-pitched sound pulsed from outside the cabin.

I thought of the Assistant Cook's last words.

The cabin was hot and humid. The front of my new coveralls was already marked with my sweat.

I opened the cabin door halfway and flapped the ragged towel in the air. I closed the door, took off all my clothes except my underwear, went back to bed.

I closed my eyes. The sound of the pumps drummed in my head.

"Beware of the wind," I heard.

The body of a man convulsed under a white sheet.

The tall woman lay on her stomach with a birthmark on her back. Leeches crawled on her skin, swollen with blood.

When a hand sprinkled salt on the leeches, they started falling off, blood dribbling where they'd been sucking.

I woke to the sound of somebody pushing another envelope under the cabin door. The sheets were drenched. I stretched my arms, lifted myself up from the bed, and climbed down. The room was messy, my clothes and notes everywhere. I wondered if the Assistant Cook was going to get tired of my mess, complain like the other people in my life.

I opened the letter, which was from the Publisher, and read:

> *Don't forget that we have a contract. Sometimes things are not ideal, but we agreed. Life is about compromise. Like in a good marriage, in good writing we meet each other halfway. It is sometimes not just about the husband and wife.*

There are always other parties to keep happy.
Make a guess!

If we need to change something so much, it
only speaks to its power. When there is fire, there
is fear. The shadows create fear, but they're the
most fearful ones. Fear necessitates compromise.

We're always there to negotiate. In the act of
negotiation, things change.

But still, it would be best to have a say in
what we want to say. No?

I'd hoped I'd do better, but the landscape
has changed. The land is dry. The winds are
strong.

Please do the edits. Time is running out.

I read the letter again. Was somebody other than the Publisher himself enforcing the edits?

At least the Publisher still believed in the book. But I wasn't ready for the compromise he was speaking of. Maybe if the book hadn't been so personal, it wouldn't have mattered to me as much. I would have done the edits he was asking for.

I put the envelope and the letter back into my suitcase. I piled all the other notes and papers in one place and folded all my clothes.

I transcribed my recordings so far and destroyed the tape. I uncovered the Assistant Cook's mattress, lifted it up. I taped the notebook with the report to the bottom of the mattress, but it kept falling off. I taped it again with as much tape as I could.

It finally stayed attached to the mattress, but it looked a mess.

Tara would always end up redoing things when I didn't do them to her standards.

I wasn't good with my hands.

I didn't know how to hold a drill. Something as simple as assembling a drawer was a nightmare.

I imagined my father as being a pretty handy person. He'd worked at a factory for many years. Maybe if I'd had him around, things would've been different.

At the same time, he wrote poetry, but all I had from him was a notebook, along with his library of books.

I arranged everything the way it'd been before.

• • •

When I left the cabin, the hallway was quiet and dim. They had shut down all the pumps.

I walked to the deck to get some air.

The sun was in the middle of the sky. All the workers were on deck. They covered their faces with their hands or scarves.

A man stood on an elevated part of the deck, a container of gasoline in his hands. Security guards surrounded him, their batons high in the air.

"This is a safety hazard — please go to your cabins," a voice said over a speaker. "You're putting all of us at risk."

The guards pushed the crowd away.

The man raised the container above his head and shivered as he poured the gasoline over himself.

The batons landed on bodies. The bodies became a river that swallowed me. I was pushed forward. I couldn't breathe. I looked back one last time and saw the red flames rising. The man ran around aflame.

I heard him scream.

My nostrils stung from the tear gas. My eyes felt like they were filled with glass shards.

The river of bodies crushed the cafeteria door. It spat me out onto the floor like something that didn't belong. I lay there. Around me shards of glass, broken plates, crushed bananas. I pulled noodles out of my beard.

The crowd had already scattered.

•   •   •

A nurse tended to some of the workers. They checked my pulse, told me I wasn't injured and could go back to my room.

Another crew was cleaning the deck and the cafeteria.

I made my way back to my cabin.

In the cabin, a man was lying on the Assistant Cook's bed.

He had a short neck and his head sank into his torso. A vein swelled under his right eye. His head was shaved.

I could hear the humming of the equipment again. The room had been cleaned. All my clothes and papers were on my suitcase.

"Nice to meet you," he said. "I hear you don't work here."

I looked around.

"Sorry, I did a little bit of housekeeping, thought the cleaners may be busy for a while."

"Where did my roommate go?" I asked. "The Assistant Cook."

"We never stay for long in one place," he said. "I hope you weren't hurt badly in the event."

I hadn't heard a helicopter landing on the deck. Hadn't they taken the burning man to a hospital?

I felt as if I had grit under my skin.

"Are you coming for dinner?" my new roommate asked. "I think the mess should be cleaned up by now."

"I'll come soon," I said. "You go ahead."

But I stayed in the cabin.

. . .

When I went to the kitchen the next day, the Assistant Cook wasn't there. Nor was the girl with the lighter.

Two unfamiliar faces were moving around the sizzling pots and pans, sweating in the heat.

"Can we help you with something?" they said. "The meals are served in the cafeteria. Not here."

I wanted to ask them if they knew where the Assistant Cook was, but I changed my mind. I already knew what this meant and what the answer was going to be.

I wondered if I would see the Assistant Cook again.

I remembered the writer friend who had disappeared from my life. The only writer friend I'd had, who'd stopped talking to me one day.

After he did not respond to my phone calls, his wife told Tara that he wasn't writing. She'd told her that he didn't want to talk to me. That I should stop calling him.

Unlike me, he'd already published three books. He was one of the few writers who wasn't tied to anybody and whose success was not a compromise.

Around the time he stopped talking to me, his books were disappearing from bookstores.

There were rumours about an illness or house arrest.

A while after that, I got the news about the publication of my own book.

I remembered I could see the mountains from anywhere in the city that day. The sun was shining.

I wasn't the grey figure separated from the sunny crowds anymore.

I decided to walk to my favourite café, which I hadn't visited in a year.

Before entering, I saw the writer's brother inside with his friends. Without knowing why, I was walking away from the café.

It would have been embarrassing if the writer's brother had noticed me.

For a long time, I tried to reach my writer friend again and again. When all my efforts failed, I started to resent him. I'd thought we were friends. He was the only person I'd shown my writing to, yet he'd decided to cut me loose just like that.

Two weeks after the day at the café, I heard the news of the writer's suicide. He'd hanged himself in his study.

I started sobbing when a friend of mine called to tell me the news.

"I can't believe it," I said to Tara, who'd come to my room after hearing me sob.

I remembered the dark curtains in his study. The smell of dust, cologne, and cigarettes in the room. His window always open, even in winter. The last time I'd met him there, he'd been coughing, but everything had seemed normal.

He said he'd liked the last excerpt from my book that I'd shown him, which had been enough to keep me going.

"Good things are ahead, B — this is really good."

I cried so much that my whole body ached.

Tara made a warm bath with bath salts and oil. She told me to get in.

"I liked him a lot, too. I can't believe that he'd do such a thing," she said. "I am so sorry for your friend, B."

When we called his wife, she told us that the funeral was limited to the closer family.

"B, I am sorry. It's best if you don't come," she said. Her voice was cold and detached, but it felt like she was withholding something from us.

* * *

When I stretched, a pain shot through my back. After the new roommate left the room, I lifted his mattress and looked underneath. The notebook was still there.

I opened it. Flipped through the pages of my report. At the other end of the notebook, I'd written something in a different handwriting. I didn't remember when I had written this.

From My Notebook

The fisherman did not want to go to the sea anymore. Whenever he went, he would fall behind the others. He could not lift the net.

When he could no longer catch any fish, they tied him up in an empty hut.

They undressed him, rubbed his skin with a mixture of rosewater, basil, and cardamom. Rubbed fish oil under his nose.

Tied his toes with goat hair.

CHAPTER 4

My mother had found my father's notebook two years after he left. She hadn't shown it to me until I was a teenager. On most of the pages, he'd described only scenes from my early childhood. How I started to move my feet, brought things to my mouth, the first words I'd said.

I didn't know why what I'd said mattered.

All the pages had dates on them, and I noticed that the notes had stopped at some point and then started up again a year later. I would've been around three by then. This time he'd written about his interactions with a homeless man who was frequenting his store.

I barely remembered the store, other than the strange smell of pesticides and herbicides that my father used to sell. I'd heard from my mother that he had difficulty paying the rent in the one year that he worked there.

My father had opened the store after he was laid off from his union job at the factory, and the store had soon become more of a hangout for his comrades and local activists. The details of the layoff weren't fully revealed to me even after the interviews I conducted with my father's former colleagues.

I learned that my father had had a leading role in the factory union when a strike started. The state had eventually interfered violently to stop the strike.

Some of my father's comrades spent time in prison around the same time, but my father wasn't arrested during the crackdown.

My mother said after opening the store, she had tried to persuade him to reduce his other activities and focus on the new business.

"Things are different — we have a kid now," my mother said.

"But I can't leave the others alone now," my father responded. "It's not only our family we're responsible for."

What I didn't understand was why my mother wasn't angry at him for this. Wasn't family one's top responsibility?

The state was sensitive to such activities in those years and his name had remained on a blacklist.

But what could a former factory worker do from his small shop that would pose such a threat to the state? I didn't understand.

"You know sometimes things were blown out of proportion — they heard a name and they associated it with something bigger. Somehow the whole discourse was shifted. Maybe some informants just exaggerated your father's role to make a deal with the state," a former colleague said. "But people were arrested, even executed, for small things in those days."

I went through the names of people who were imprisoned and released soon after around that time, but couldn't find something that would link them to him.

"Your father was more influential than some of us knew," another comrade said. "He connected multiple unions together. That was the state's main fear. I can see how that could have had more serious consequences. Not just a couple of years in prison."

"Your father had no fear," my mother said. "It was only when we were at risk that he decided to leave."

But all of these seemed more like speculations.

Why did my father write about the homeless man so much and never anything about himself or these events?

At the store, my father would make the homeless man tea and they would play chess together.

As a child, the homeless man had been abused by his big brothers. They'd urinated on him, had made him watch them fuck a prostitute.

My father had lost his own father when he was ten. Unlike the homeless man, he didn't have any brothers.

The notebook had become a dream log after that, describing my father's dreams.

• • •

After the Assistant Cook disappeared, I spent most of my days in the cabin reading *The Book of the Winds*, the old book I had brought with me, or dozing on my remaining stash of sleeping pills. I felt numb.

I was afraid to interview new people or work on the report.
I sometimes walked around the hallways, or made my way
to other rooms — kitchen, gym, TV room, control room —
thinking I might run into someone who would talk to me. But
I couldn't always get into all of the rooms.

No one talked to me.

Obviously, I wasn't wanted there.

I had witnessed something, though I didn't know what it
was. I didn't know what exactly had happened to the burnt
man or the Assistant Cook.

In theory I could've left, but I still hoped to find out something more.

The Editor no longer emailed me, asking for updates.
What I had so far, after a month on the rig, was my interview
with the Assistant Cook, some notes on my general observations, and my report on the event where the man had set
himself on fire. The pieces didn't come together yet, and it
probably wasn't enough to justify my trip, to generate the
expected report.

If I went back earlier than planned, the Editor might think
I hadn't done all I could. They could've asked me to give them
back the advance if they weren't satisfied with the report. But
that wasn't why I stayed.

I didn't know what else I could do under the circumstances.
I just wasn't prepared to leave.

The new roommate didn't come back to the cabin other
than to sleep at night.

I tried to sit with others a couple of times during meals, but
everybody fell silent when they saw me, staring at their plates.

I didn't know if the management had warned them about
me, or they just didn't trust me on their own.

After that I sat alone, trying to finish my meals quickly so I could go back to my cabin.

I would have taken something to my room if they let me, but you weren't supposed to do that.

I kept looking for the men who used to greet the Assistant Cook. But none of the faces looked familiar anymore.

Tara hadn't written in a while and I noticed that I had completely lost my connection to the outside world.

My room didn't have a TV. In the TV room, roughnecks would get mad if anyone tried to change it from the comedy channel. It was where they went to hang out, though they mostly dozed, or played dice without talking to each other.

If there was a war going on, or someone was dead, I probably wouldn't have known.

•   •   •

It was midday when I woke and saw somebody in the cabin, standing beside my suitcase. The room was dark.

"Who're you?" I screamed.

"Sorry, sorry," she said. "Just cleaning your room. I didn't turn on the lights because I didn't want to wake you."

I had been dreaming of my father before I woke.

We were hiking on a snowy hill when a policeman on a black horse appeared. Before I knew it, the man took out a pistol and shot my father.

My father laughed as he rolled down the fresh snow.

A splash of red on white.

I could still hear the trotting of the horse.

She turned on the lights and came closer to the bed.

"Would you let me change your sheets? The room is getting a little stuffy."

"Has my roommate complained?"

"No, just I am supposed to do it, but you're mostly in bed, so I have been skipping it."

I stepped down the ladder and stood there while she changed the sheets on my bed.

She sprayed the air with an air freshener that smelled of pine.

"Sorry, the cabin isn't ventilated," she said. "You shouldn't be sleeping so much."

She opened the mini-fridge and placed four bottles of water inside it.

"I have left you a garbage bag. You can put your garbage by the door every day. See that basket over there — you can leave your dirty laundry there."

"Have you talked with your husband recently?" I asked her.

"Why do you ask that?" she said.

"Just that I haven't talked to anyone for a while. I don't even know if everything is as it was before."

"Why shouldn't it be? Everything is always the same," she said. "Remember I told you that I don't call him."

"I remember," I said.

She said, "I hope they haven't haunted your dreams."

Was she referring to the bad spirits that rode on the winds? I was a little surprised by this remark, but I didn't take it seriously. I was hoping to learn something more from her.

"The man who killed himself," I said, trying to open the conversation about something the Assistant Cook had mentioned.

"You're scaring me."

She quickly grabbed her cleaning supplies from the room and stepped toward the door, but then she came back. She touched the four corners of the room before she left and chanted an incantation.

Her chant reminded me of the night of the ceremony on my way to the rig, the smells in the air, the women in veils, the white cloth.

It all seemed so far away.

"You should stop reading that book," the cleaning lady said, looking at *The Book of the Winds* on my bed. "That's probably what's messing with your head."

From *The Book of the Winds*

Menmendas appears as a young and beautiful woman with long black hair. She has a jewellery box that she always carries with her. Men easily fall for her and follow her.

She leads them to old ruins or deserted places to lie with them. She places the jewellery box under her head, lies on the ground, and opens her legs. If the man is tempted and attempts to lie with her, her thighs turn into sharp saws that butcher the man into halves. If the man recognizes Menmendas, he has to throw a fistful of dirt at her face, take the jewellery box, and run away.

The helicopter hadn't been on the platform in a while. I wasn't sure if something had changed on the mainland or it was just the events on the rig.

That was when I decided to talk to the boy.

Whenever I understood the roughnecks, they were talking about losing time because of maintenance issues.

Despite the lower demand, a minute of stoppage in production still meant huge sums of money.

The men were talking about problems with getting the replacement parts in time.

They threw words like *backlog* or *supply chain* at each other.

They talked about losing money as if it was their money.

They complained about somebody not doing his job.

They talked about someone being a rat.

They never talked about those who disappeared or left.

The boy sometimes sat alone during meals. I had seen him on the deck, cleaning oil sludge from the pipes, blowing air into the dirty vessels, or pressure-washing them.

I looked at the sky and the ocean. The clouds took the shape of monsters. The wind moved the monsters around to different rigs, to different lands.

The platform wobbled in its place, the waves high.

The boy had a frail figure, tanned skin, a ponytail.

That night during dinner, he was sitting with another man, but the man wasn't even looking at him. After dinner I followed the boy through the network of pipes, walking at a distance from him.

The night staff still hadn't shown up on the deck. The sky was scarred with red lines. Pelicans dived against the angry waves.

When it grew darker, I didn't turn on my flashlight. I could see the boy's long shadow moving on the deck. I continued moving at a distance from him.

Behind a tank, the boy suddenly turned and jumped on me. I hit my back against a steel vessel and fell. He kneeled on the ground, pressed my neck with one hand, and pulled my hair with the other.

I noticed how long my hair had grown. There was a pressure at the back of my skull as he pulled.

He let go of my hair but kept pressing on my neck.

He pulled a small leather pendant out of his shirt and took from it a folded parchment with a spell written on it. He unfolded the spell and chanted something.

I couldn't breathe well. I coughed.

"What the fuck do you want?" he said. "You're always looking at me like that, and now you're following me."

"Nothing," I said. "I just wanted to talk to you."

"You fucking freak. I have nothing to talk to you about."

He spat on my face and let me go. I was cleaning my face when a flashlight lit our faces.

"Is everything all right?" a guard asked.

The boy walked away as soon as he saw the guard.

I hadn't seen this guard on the rig before.

I leaned on the vessel to stand up, then slowly made my way to my room.

I couldn't do much when these people didn't trust me.

I didn't blame them for not trusting someone who wasn't one of them.

I wondered if they blamed me for the disappearance of the Assistant Cook.

. . .

The next day, I went to the reception desk. It had been a long time since I had gone there.

"There are no letters for you," the Secretary said. "We will send them to your cabin if there are any."

"That's okay," I said. "I just want to go home. I was wondering if you can book me in for the next helicopter?"

"I am afraid that won't be possible."

"Why?" I asked.

"We have a huge backlog right now — a lot of workers still need to be moved around, and we still don't have an estimate of when the next one will be here."

"Are you telling me I am stuck here? I thought they wanted me gone."

"I can certainly put you on the wait-list. Would you want me to do that?"

"Please!"

. . .

I was reading in my bed when the cabin door opened and a man came in. Half of his face looked deflated.

"It burns. It burns," he shouted.

He switched the lights off, took my water bottle out of the mini-fridge, and emptied it onto his head.

"What are you doing here?"

"Shut up! You don't understand."

"How did you get in?"

His teeth chattered.

He took a second bottle from the fridge and drank it.

He opened my suitcase and threw my clothes onto the floor as if he was searching for something.

"You can't do that," I said. "What are you even looking for?"

He put his ear against the door. "They're here. Shut up!" He crawled under the bed.

"You can't be here," I said.

He started squealing like a sea lion, crawled out and ran out of the room, slamming the door behind him.

Several minutes after he left, I checked underneath the bed.

My notebook was still there.

I unlocked the door and looked into the hallway but didn't see anyone.

I locked the door again.

From *The Book of the Winds*

Whereas sometimes the spirit may leave the body, the wind may stay behind in the head and need more blood and ceremony to depart.

Before the ceremony, a woman goes around the village with a bamboo cane and invites the people of the wind by knocking at their doors. Many invitees are young girls who have soft voices and smooth moves and wear dresses that give colour to the ceremony.

All the people of the wind have been possessed before and defeated their wind at least once in the past.

The father of the wind plays the biggest drum with at least two other men playing smaller drums and pipes.

Some winds require a larger ceremony and more blood to be spilled for the wind to be exorcised.

Empty hallways. Flickering lights. The body of a woman on the floor, bare legs bruised.

I felt a body pressing against my chest. A light went through me.

Through the light, I saw the man with the deflated face attached to a rope, trying to rise to the surface of the water, big air bubbles coming out of his mouth.

I heard myself scream. I woke breathless, half of my body numb. I couldn't move my right arm.

When I didn't go for lunch the next day, the cleaning woman brought me food.

"I was worried this might happen," she said.

She persuaded me to see the doctor first, but said that it likely wouldn't work.

Later in the day, she knocked at the cabin's door. "The doctor is ready to see you."

I followed her through the hallways to a dark room I had not seen before.

The room had a view of the ocean and smelled of rubbing alcohol.

It was hazy outside and I could see the black clouds swirling at a distance from the platform.

The doctor had a long narrow face, with short white hair, and frameless glasses. He wore an orange safety vest. A stethoscope hung from his neck.

"Push my hands," the Doctor said. "The Wind." The Doctor laughed. "The locals say it brings bad spirits.

"Long work hours and little pay," he said. "Wife sleeping with your brother when you're away."

He stroked underneath my left knee with a rubber hammer.

"One can spend a lifetime naming the winds."

"It doesn't react as much on the left." He pointed at my knee.

"Nothing major," he said.

"What about the heaviness in my chest?" I asked.

"No significance," he said. "Don't listen to what these people say. It's out of their helplessness that they make these things up. You've been reading too much about southern folks.

"They may think you're possessed by the winds and avoid you." He laughed.

"Just go back home!" he said. "Everything will go away when you are in bed with your wife again."

I didn't tell him that I wanted to, but I couldn't.

From My Notebook

When the people of the wind couldn't tame the fisherman's wind, his mother had to make a larger sacrifice. But that wasn't enough. The untamed wind had driven him to complete madness. His wind followed him like a wild beast running behind him. Always hungry.

Children threw stones at him to keep him away. He had to leave town, had to hunt for his food or find it in dumpsters like a stray dog.

Tied to a deserted shrine in the middle of the desert. His bones were jabbing out of his flesh. He was licking a bowl of curdled milk somebody had left in front of him.

Following the visit with the doctor, I was still limping. My right hand didn't have enough strength, but I was able to turn it into a fist again. A pain started from the tip of my fingers and shot up to my neck. I kept twisting my head, trying to reduce the pain.

Words were blurry around the edges.

At night I dreamed of dirty pools of water. I came to the surface, choking. I was naked, trying to hide something from the people who were after me.

My beard had grown long, with more white strands appearing.

I left the cabin and limped under the sun. My skin had changed colour and itched, patches of it turning into small flakes that I'd strip away at night in my bed.

I might have gotten used to the noise. The workers on deck ignored me. They were at work as if nothing had happened.

One of the workers had lit himself on fire. New workers had replaced those who were there that day.

They all looked alike. Numbers on hard hats. No names.

Maybe the former workers had all just gone somewhere else.

. . .

I should've known that the new roommate was there only to watch me. I wasn't actively working on the report and just wanted the trip to be over, then. My previous encounters hadn't led to anything, and I didn't trust the roommate to begin with.

It started with me talking about being on the wait-list, wanting to go home. He said he was tired of being on the rig himself. He hadn't seen his family for six weeks and he was due for a trip back.

This was probably when I thought he might be open to talking more. When I asked him about the strikes, he pretended that such a thing didn't exist.

To his knowledge, the case of the burnt man had been a result of mental illness, drugs smuggled into the rig.

He'd always worked hard, received his money on time, and most of the workers were similar to him. Well, there were some layoffs, as the demand for oil was less now, but the Company always maintained the good workers despite everything.

I became quiet as he said these things. I realized that I had made a mistake in talking to him.

It was right after asking him about the strikes that I received the package.

From *The Book of the Winds*

The spirits can be anywhere, but they mainly wait under Banyan trees, around water wells. Under the sea.

They're more likely to hunt down the hungry, the thirsty. They reside where fear grows.

Sometimes the signs of possession start with a simple itching or burning that gradually spreads to all body parts. The skin bloats, and the possessed may try to peel off their own skin.

Other times the possession starts with strange dreams. The possessed may dream of mutilated bodies following them, or of being choked.

The skin becomes pale and the eyes go gaunt. The possessed sleep, cry, and resist bathing.

Sometimes the possessed cannot move. The teeth lock and the mouth foams.

The possessed speak with a different voice or even a different dialect that may not be known to others.

That I had been selected to write the report. That I had accepted it without much doubt.

That the Editor had emailed me one day out of nowhere. That he'd got my contact information from the Publisher. That he hadn't met me at the agency's office or a café, but asked me to come to his private office.

That the office had been in an industrial area near a plastic mould factory, which had surprised me. It didn't have its own bathroom and I had to go to the factory to pee. That the smell of burnt plastic had been strong. In the bathroom, the rusted lockers and dirtiness had reminded me of bathrooms at school.

That the Editor had made it all seem simple at the time: "Just be there. Take notes, describe what you see." But there had been other expectations.

That it had all seemed strange, but I had accepted it.

That I had only wanted to change things. That I had hoped this would help change things.

•　•　•

The sea swelling. Exhaust gas flaring toward the sky. Surrounded on all sides by water.

The wind wailing.

Smell of oil, sulphur, and burnt waste.

The monstrous metallic cranes moving up and down.

Islands and other rigs visible on sunny days. But most days, the sun like a lamp in a steam room.

Sometimes I could smell the palm trees from miles away. The gulls gathered when the plant waste was dumped into the sea.

My mouth had a bitter, salty taste.

Drunk roughnecks vomited into the ocean, the wind spattering their vomit. Their eyes red from exhaustion or drugs.

Dark clouds under the eyes. Dark clouds in the sky.

The waves rolled. The hallways circled around.

Cormorants made a black wave through the sky.

Most days I forgot where I was.

Fishing boats in the distance went home without any catch.

Workers watched comedy shows. Their teeth tore into steaks. Fish fillets. Drumsticks.

Plates were cleaned with bread.

Men threw dice. They dozed by the TV, by screens. They dozed while eating dinner.

They drilled, torqued, welded, and cleaned.

They dived in deep with capsules of oxygen.

Men drank water.

Other men were thirsty.

Women were thirsty.

· · ·

My notebook was still under the mattress.

The package that I'd received included a picture of me and the woman from the bookstore whom I'd followed back to her apartment.

Both of us naked on her bed. Our faces blackened by a marker. Even without that, it was probably hard to recognize me from that angle, but likely they had more images. Possibly even videos.

I remembered the muddy footprints on our kitchen floor, several days before my encounter with the tall woman. Tara had thought I'd entered the house with my boots on. She did not believe me when I denied it.

I showed her my boots. There was no mud, but she still didn't believe me.

I checked every corner of the house. All the locks and windows. Nothing had been touched, let alone taken.

A week before that, the window of our car had been smashed.

I told her these events were related.

"You reek of alcohol. Have you been drinking?" she asked. "What's going on with you?" She held my head between her hands. "Look at me."

I remembered the unfamiliar smell of her hands. Something fruity and sweet. It wasn't her perfume.

"Is this about the house? If this is about the house —"

The house was unfamiliar, unfriendly. I didn't feel good that I had no share in paying for it.

Neighbours kept asking questions about what I was doing, what I was going to do.

I looked at the bare branches of a walnut tree all day. I heard noises from inside the walls.

Words appeared on the page.

I didn't know where I was being taken to.

"It's not the house," I said.

I looked into her eyes. Weren't they supposed to show something more?

She pressed my head to her chest.

I kept looking for what was missing. On her skin. I dipped my nose into her collar and couldn't breathe it in.

"I'll go for a drive," I said.

She went to the bedroom and slammed the door.

The windshield wipers thudded as I drove. I took my flask out of my jacket pocket and sipped. I didn't remember when the rain had started.

• • •

The Secretary had handed me the package. I wondered if they had a photo that showed the tall woman's face. I remembered her small mouth, the strange colour of her lips. I looked at the photo over and over. The white sheets tinted yellow.

Sometimes I imagined that it hadn't actually happened.

You opened the door to somebody else's apartment — before you knew it, you were in the middle of another life. Maybe it resembled a life you'd decided to call your own.

I looked small against the tall windows of her room. My hairy back faced the camera. The wind lifted the white curtains.

That a small detail could lead me to something new, help me remember something I'd forgotten.

It had sounded strange that she had picked up my favourite novel, but there hadn't been any other books in her apartment. That she had been interested in me even without talking to me.

I couldn't sleep after I ran out of the remaining sleeping pills.

Tara didn't write back. I stopped sending her messages.

I deserved it all.

• • •

Finally, I received an email. To my surprise, it wasn't from Tara or the Editor, but from my Publisher. In the next chapter he'd sent me, he hadn't used a red pen for his edits. My meaning had been dissolved into whatever he'd added. I no longer recognized the words. This time, there were not even any photos of my father. There was the following note from the Publisher:

> *I am thinking we should call this a novel, since I*
> *have taken some liberty with the material.*

In this version of the text, my father was only a man selling herbicides. He had lost his father when he was ten.

He didn't have a past.

He never led a union at the factory or was laid off.

He was just in a bad marriage. Maybe he was gay.

He wasn't an activist.

He was only going through a mid-life crisis.

He had stopped writing poetry.

He might have just fled the country and remarried.

He might have fled the country and killed himself.

He might not even have left the country.

Maybe he was just afraid.

My mother had told me time and time again that the state had spread rumours about my father, portraying him as a closeted queer who had run away from his family. They were just to stain his name and other activists connected to him. Make him look petty, like he wasn't even brave enough to defend his own identity.

No one even knew or cared that he'd existed.

Few former colleagues and comrades.

My mother and I.

A successful erasure of him.

My failure to change that.

• • •

"Too bad you're not finishing your memoir," the Secretary said. "I loved your writing."

I was so displaced that I hadn't noticed I had sat across from the Secretary and read the whole revised chapter right there.

"I've read your two chapters multiple times," she added. "My roommate and I both love it. It's so creative, the way you write about your father."

"Thank you," I said. I felt like a stranger had opened my drawer and rearranged my underwear. Other than my writer friend and the Publisher, nobody had read the book. Not even Tara.

"I want to go back with the first available helicopter," I said. "Please, I am ready to go back."

My voice came out so weak I wasn't sure she had heard it.

"Actually, I was about to give you some news in that regard. We've been informed that the next helicopter should be here in two days. You're pretty high up on the list," she said. "I'll see what I can do."

The sharp angles of her face softened to give way to a sadness. She wrote something on a notepad, shielding the note from the camera behind her with her hands.

But there are things you don't know, she wrote. *Meet me at my cabin after dinner.*

Her cabin number was written on the note.

• • •

When the Secretary opened the door, she was in a pink silk robe. She didn't have any makeup on.

Her cabin had a tropical smell that contrasted with the rugged atmosphere of the rig. I wondered what had changed her hostility toward me. Being in the cabin and sitting on her tiny bed felt strange.

How had I even agreed to be here, after all that had happened? I was still desperate for the clues to add up to something, for my trip to lead to a conclusion. I had to follow any potential lead until I was off the rig.

I wondered if things might have gone differently if I had gone to another rig or stayed in the refinery.

"What did you want to tell me?" I asked impatiently, my eyes moving over the objects in the cabin.

"Do you think you're ready to hear it?"

"Yes."

"I've been keeping some of your mail."

"Why?"

"I didn't feel you were in a good enough state to receive the news."

"And why are you telling me this now?"

"I thought you needed to know before you make a decision."

She handed me a piece of paper. "This is what they sent you."

I took it from her hand. It was a scan of a handwritten letter. The handwriting was Tara's.

> It is weird to have you at our house. I woke up excited this morning after so many years, watched the sunrise. How we stop seeing things. Everything becomes flat and sad.
> Sorry for making you sleep in the guest room. I don't want to mix things up.

*You're only a room away, probably sleep-
ing, but I already miss you. I can smell you in
my bed. I'll sleep in the guest room with you
tonight.*

*Maybe it's time to sell this house and put the
past behind me.*

I crumpled up the paper. I wondered who the man or the
woman in our guest room was.

I couldn't believe it. Had my previous suspicion been cor-
rect? Or had things changed after I left?

I remembered Tara, smiling as she was reading something
on her phone.

I remembered her on the day I left. Her eyes wet.

I heard her steps as she was coming up the stairs — we were
both young.

Our bodies floated in the lake. The reflection of the clouds
on the water.

I recognized her handwriting, but couldn't they have forged
her words?

When I wept, the Secretary held me. I could taste the salt
of my tears.

I pictured Tara in our bedroom.

I pictured the stranger in our guest room.

I knew I deserved this, if it was real.

"I'm sorry," I said.

"It's okay," the Secretary said, caressing my head.

"Do you know who sent this letter to me?"

"It was from an unknown email address. An attachment.
Nothing was written in the body of the email."

I looked at the scanned letter again.

"Are you sure it's her handwriting?" the Secretary asked.

"I think so."

She coughed and moved to the other end of the bed.

"You'd better be back in your room before your roommate goes to sleep," she said. "They'll become suspicious otherwise. I'll see you tomorrow. We'll see what happens with the helicopter."

But I wasn't as sure that I wanted to leave anymore. What was I going back to?

She'd kept the cabin door half open and watched me as I limped away.

The hallway curved until I could no longer see her.

When I got back to the room, my roommate wasn't there.

I sat on my bed and hugged my knees.

Maybe they'd replicated her handwriting. It wouldn't be hard to do.

They did everything they could to separate you from everybody else.

I climbed down off the bed and lifted my roommate's mattress.

The notebook was missing.

They'd probably planned this to make sure I was out of the cabin long enough for them to search the room.

I immediately left my cabin to go back to the Secretary's room.

I knocked but she didn't open this time.

I checked the number on the door. It was the same number.

"Open up," I shouted, knocking again.

After a while, a roughneck opened the door, rubbing his eyes.

"What the fuck do you want? I'm trying to sleep," he said, squinting in the hallway light.

He was in his underpants. His chest and shoulders were covered with curls of black hair.

The Secretary had played me. I'd been played since the beginning.

I dragged myself back to my cabin.

I have to get out of this place, I thought.

I thought of all who had disappeared: my father, my writer friend, the woman in the bookstore, the Assistant Cook.

I thought of the girl with the lighter, whom I hadn't seen again.

I remembered what the Assistant Cook had said on our last night together.

I kept twisting and turning in the bed, checking the time. From the hallway, I heard whispers over the humming of the equipment, but maybe I was imagining the voices.

What would the morning bring? I asked myself.

I might've dozed for several minutes and woke when another envelope was pushed inside. I left the bed and opened it.

> *You didn't tell me that the publication date has been pushed forward.*
>
> *We can't even celebrate the good things together anymore?*
>
> *The cover looks great! I'll read it soon.*
>
> *Miss you,*
> *Tara*

I couldn't understand what she was talking about.

When there were so many lies, how could you distinguish the truth?

My eyelids were heavy. I hadn't slept much in a long time. I thought I'd go onto the deck before going to the cafeteria to get some coffee. I'd come back and try to recreate the report.

But when I opened the door, two security guards were waiting there for me.

I first heard the propeller when they tied my hands and covered my eyes. They guided me to the deck after but didn't take me to the helicopter.

The morning air was cold. I didn't know what was waiting for me.

I heard gulls calling among the humming of machines. The guards whispered to each other, pushed me somewhere that smelled of metal and fresh paint.

A door banged behind me and was bolted. A chain was pulled, and the beeping of the crane began.

"Up, up, up," a voice shouted in the distance.

The ground tilted underneath me.

I lost my balance, rolled to the side, hitting a hard surface with my elbows.

I covered my head with my arms. I crumpled into a ball, tried to find something to hold onto.

I screamed, "Help," and heard my screaming echo.

The motion stopped, and after several minutes, the door opened. Hands lifted me and held my arms, led me to a cooler space. We walked up several stairs, then took more steps.

They removed my blindfold but didn't untie my hands. When I opened my eyes, I was in an office-looking cabin in a ship. It was much bigger than the cabins in the rig. Two new guards had replaced the two who had arrested me.

A man with long white hair was sitting behind a desk, facing me. Bony face. Angular jaw.

I could see the reflection of the room in his circular glasses.

The guards made me sit in a chair.

The cabin had windows that faced the ocean. I could see the cranes and the platform. We were on a cargo ship with colourful c-cans stacked on top of each other on the deck.

We were slowly moving away from the rig. The hydrocarbon smell faded, the loud noises gone.

The room was silent. The two guards and the man didn't move.

In one corner of the room, there was a shelf with books. I couldn't read the titles from where I was.

"I hear you're writing a book," the man behind the desk said.

I was surprised by the first thing he said.

"Why am I here?" I asked.

"Why do you think you're here?"

I remembered the meeting with the Editor.

Tara waving to me at the door, her eyes wet.

The wounded cows and the man convulsing under a white cloth.

The man with the deflated face.

The photo of me and the woman from the bookstore.

I couldn't believe that all these things had happened.

"Look! I'd like to know where I am being taken. I need to let my wife know where I am. She'll be very worried."

"It's good to see that you are showing concern for others." He paused, then asked, "When was the last time you contacted her?"

I didn't know how to answer this. I hadn't contacted her for several weeks, at least. I hadn't even looked at a calendar in a long time.

I looked into his eyes, but he was looking down at his notebook. I noticed his shoes underneath his desk. They were old shoes, but well polished and clean.

I was barefoot. Why wasn't I wearing my boots?

Nobody was wearing steel-toed boots here. The room was air-conditioned.

"I guess I'm here because of the report," I said when he didn't say anything. "But you already have the report. It was stolen from my cabin yesterday."

He still didn't talk. But he'd started by talking about the book.

So, I said, "Or maybe because of the book that I've written."

"I am glad to tell you that your book is published," the man said. His eyes still didn't look directly at me. When he talked, only his lips moved.

He had curly eyelashes. His voice sounded like stones rubbing against each other.

"I don't know if it is published," I said. "The two chapters I've seen had little to do with what I wrote."

"Maybe that's for the best," he said. "But I am telling you that it's published. You should be happy now."

The man then scribbled things in his notebook. He waited, looking down at his notes again.

"It's a big deal, being published these days," he continued.

"Look! I was supposed to write a report to make some money. I had no idea that you didn't want me —"

"I didn't want?" he asked. "Why do you think I would care?"

The guards, who had not moved at all until then, standing like statues, chuckled.

"I didn't know what I was doing. Now you have my report. You have seen that it's limited to my personal observations. I was planning to go back, anyways. I had informed the Secretary. You can ask her. I've been waiting for a helicopter to go back for a while now. I don't want any trouble."

"Yes, we're aware of the logistical issues. But those are not important. These things happen. Bad weather. Natural disasters. They don't get in our way. We're more worried about you," he added. "You've been suffering."

For a moment, I felt sympathy in his voice.

"If so, shouldn't you let me go back to my life? I don't know why I'm here. Nobody is really benefitting from this."

"You'll go back. When you're better," the man said. "This may not be as bad as you think. We're here to help. Since you didn't seek it yourself, we had to intervene. There is a lot of sensitivity here. Belief in superstitious practices. But we tend to stick with science."

"The doctor can certify that I am fine. I just need to go back home. You can speak to him."

"We have all the information we need. You don't need to worry too much. Things will follow their due course now."

"But I had permission. I haven't done anything illegal." I remembered that nothing in my suitcase, including the stamped letter, was with me.

"The agency knows exactly where I was," I said. "They acquired a permit."

"Have you communicated with the agency recently?" he asked. "Let me put it another way. Have you communicated with anyone but your editor at the agency? As he is no longer part of the agency."

I hadn't talked to anyone else at the agency. I hadn't heard back from the Editor in a while.

"Not to mention that things can change. What is considered innocent today may not be so tomorrow. But this isn't about one thing or another. You've had enough opportunities to prove us wrong, but you haven't yet. It may take longer now, but you'll still have chances."

I tried to stand up, but I couldn't feel my legs. I was about to fall when the guards caught me. They made me sit back down in the chair again.

"We have a lot to talk about. I am especially excited to hear more about the book, but it seems you've had enough for today." He said to the guards, "Help him."

They lifted me under my arms and hauled me down the empty hallway.

The hallway spiralled around. The air had a strong smell of disinfectant and sweat.

On the deck, I heard the muffled barking of dogs. The row of c-cans closest to the cabins was only one stack high. There was some empty space in between, and the rest of the ship's deck was stacked with multiple rows of c-cans.

In my c-can, there was a bed with a white leather mattress, a toilet seat, and a water tap in a corner. I wondered if they were piped to anywhere.

A red notebook and a pen were on the bed.

The guard turned off the lamp. As he closed the door, the narrow block of light from outside shrank until I was surrounded by darkness.

•　•　•

When I woke, an empty food tray was on the floor. The lamp hanging from the ceiling was on. My hands were untied.

I had no idea what time of day it was. I didn't remember eating any food.

The red notebook was on my chest. I had changed my clothes and drooled onto the shirt I was wearing.

I opened the notebook and looked at it. I recognized my father's pages. His handwriting.

I hadn't even brought the notebook with me to the South. I tried to remember the last time I had seen the notebook, wondering if they'd broken into the house after I'd left, or before.

I flipped through the pages and couldn't find the part about the homeless man — the part about my childhood and growing up.

The cover looked as I remembered it. They had cut the part about my childhood. They had cut the part about the homeless man.

They had left only my father's dreams.

My mouth was dry. I put my forehead against the door. The sound of the ocean echoed like when you put an empty shell to your ear.

I thought of my father alone in a room. In another land. Somewhere no one knew. His name erased. His life forgotten.

I lay on the bed. Stood again. Walked around the c-can. I was aware of my every breath. I put my hands on the walls, which were cooler to my touch now.

I banged on the walls, hoping something would give. I looked for any opening through which I could see the outside.

"Let me go," I shouted.

I lay on the bed, read through my father's dreams.

I thought about how I had ended up here.

I thought about Tara. Tried to imagine what she would be doing now. But I didn't even know where she was.

I hoped that she was safe, wished that I could go back home again.

Then the lamp turned off, and my eyes searched for all I had lost in the darkness.

●　●　●

When I woke next, there was a typed page placed on top of a pile of white pages. I wasn't sure how long had passed.

The text on the page was excerpted from my father's notebook:

> *He looked into my eyes today and smiled.*
> *When I was changing him today, he stretched his arm and held my thumb with his little fingers.*

He recognizes both me and his mother.
He presses his lips and imitates the sound
of a kiss.
He shies away from strangers and is sensitive
to the sound of music.

I rewrote the same sentences over and over.

I drew a map of the rig on another page.

At some point, the door opened and a narrow stream of light came in. I squinted and saw a guard standing outside.

It was hard to distinguish one guard from another. They all had the same blank faces.

The guard tied my hands and pulled me outside with the rope. I didn't resist, walking behind him.

The sky was overcast. The wind brushed against the colourful c-cans. I could see only a narrow view of the ocean. When we entered the cabin, the white-haired man stood and stretched with his arms in the air. Several piles of paper were neatly placed on his desk.

This time I sat in the chair without the guards forcing me to.

The room was quiet until the white-haired man spoke. "The more you write, the easier it gets," the Interrogator said.

He didn't have any accent, so I assumed he was from the city. If I saw him at a café or on the street, I could've mistaken him for an artist or a professor at one of the city universities.

I wondered if he had any children, even grandchildren.

"I expect more from someone who is a published writer." He laughed. "Some days we just give you a bit of a hint, to get you going. But our expectation is that you'd go beyond that.

"Let's look here." He flipped through the pages. "No new words today. That's okay. It means we'll have to work harder.

"Do you have something else to discuss while we're here?" he said.

When I didn't say anything, he slapped the air, which implied the guards should take me back to the c-can, to a new pile of white pages.

• • •

At first I resisted the temptation to write anything.

But I wasn't able to talk to anyone. In a dark room all day. Smell of rust and my own sweat.

The voices in my head getting louder. My thoughts a tangled mass.

The room got scorching hot in the afternoon. The sweat burned between my thighs. At night I shivered from the cold, nothing to cover myself with. I heard the waves crashing against the ship.

For a couple of days, I didn't eat the food or drink the water they brought in. I wasn't sure what they added to it. It had made me sleep long hours, and I'd woken not remembering what had happened. Things had moved around. My clothes had changed. New bruises on my body.

But my head hurt so much after two days. My lips parched. My throat so dry I couldn't swallow.

In a state of delirium, I heard voices, people talking in dialect. I didn't know if I was asleep or awake. I had these visions, or maybe they were dreams, in which people called for my help. Fishermen. Pearl hunters. The man with the deflated face. I had to find where they were. I heard their deep cries from under the sea, traced their footsteps on a deserted island.

The visions kept repeating even after I started drinking water. I didn't know what they meant. They were a word puzzle in a language you didn't understand. A word puzzle that kept changing as you looked at it, the words dissolving and smudging your fingers.

I wrote some pages in that state.

Sometimes a guard banged on the wall as soon as I went to sleep. They left the lamp on only while I was writing.

In the darkness, I couldn't read what I had written myself.

The only other light was a red dot from the surveillance camera in the corner of the c-can.

I didn't know if what I wrote meant anything.

At first I chewed and swallowed any page I wrote before the guards could retrieve it. But they watched me on the camera, coming in as soon as I finished a paragraph. They pulled it out before I had a chance to swallow.

Only when there was enough of an accumulation of words would they take me to meet with the Interrogator.

On the deck, I looked at the sky, tried to guess where the ship was going from the position of the sun and stars.

Through the narrow gaps, I would see islands of coral reefs sticking out of the sea, sparse populations of palm trees on the islands.

They all looked alike.

But I didn't come across any other rigs.

To make things more difficult on me, they stopped the water to the toilet bowl. They didn't bring in any toilet paper. When I had to go to the bathroom, I would thump at the door, but sometimes the guards wouldn't come in time and I would have to go right there.

Swarms of flies and mosquitoes buzzed around. A terrible smell in the air. I scratched myself in disgust, tried to pile my dirty clothes in one corner of the room.

Only if I wrote enough would they take me to the office, which meant the guards would hose me down with sea water on the deck. The water was cold and its high pressure made me fall down. They stood at a distance from me, wearing masks, wetsuits, and long black boots. They kicked me in the sides to make me turn around. They gave me clean clothes afterward.

Every time I returned from the visits, the floor and the leather mattress had been cleaned. The toilet bowl flushed. The c-can smelled of bleach again. A pile of paper and a pen were on the bed. I wrote more to increase the frequency of my trips.

•   •   •

Some days the prompts were typed. Some days they were hand-written; the handwriting looked like my own.

From My Notes

He couldn't remember his life before that.
Days and hours, light and darkness.
He would go into a dreamless sleep for seconds — a whiteness like death — until the man pulled a rope and dumped the bucket of ice water on him.
He was feverish and falling. His skin no longer felt the cold.

Interrogator's Questions

"You wrote a book about him, but you don't seem to know much about your father," the Interrogator said.

"Why did you choose to write this book?"

"Who were you trying to harm other than yourself?"

"Are you naive or do you think we're naive?"

"You want me to believe all of this is an accident?"

"Why did you interview the ornithologists?"

"If you can't talk, you can write it down."

"How did you get in touch with the Editor?"

"Maybe you were naive enough to trust the Editor, after all."

"Write down: *I am a coward and conspirator like my father.*"

"The Editor has *fled* the country, like your father."

"If only you had started collaborating with us earlier in your life."

From My Notes

When the ship got close to the island, it became a haven for winds and spirits. At night he could hear screams in different dialects and voices.

Fishermen and workers woke him up and led him through the marshes to the island.

They had soot-covered faces and burnt eyelashes. They stroked their drums and drank water from the well, wore white clothes and danced.

In the mirror, he looked more and more like his father.

He was looking for a ship to take him back to where he had come from.

From My Notes

The leaves of the trees were made of ash and the sun rays were grey.

He was a prophet and he had eaten God.

They found him bloated in a fishing net and they needed his blood.

His blood tasted of hydrocarbon and lead and nobody could drink it.

God screamed inside him, but the voice didn't leave his esophagus.

Fishermen searched for God with their hook-shaped hands.

"I can see that you're trying to avoid writing about what we ask. But you're writing about it without writing about it. That's the beauty of the process," the Interrogator said.

•   •   •

Every time I brought up calling Tara with the Interrogator, they stopped the conversation short, took me back to the c-can.

"I don't know why you want to call your wife," the Interrogator said.

"I don't think she would have much interest in hearing from you," he said. "Unless your book is doing really well out there."

He laughed. His chest wheezed and he coughed into a napkin to clear his lungs.

"Not all women are as good as your mother at living with lies."

"As you may guess, your wife is enjoying her new life."

"She doesn't have the same problems with her new lover."

"Imagine when she learns who you really are. The things you've done."

"What did you expect would happen?"

"Don't worry. You can always find somebody else. When you go back, there'll be other opportunities."

"The reality is you need our help more than we need yours."

I remembered the time I had planned a trip to a river town with Tara. It was after the news about the book's acceptance. Our last trip together.

I had heard there was a beautiful river there, which we could bike alongside. I had rented two bicycles.

When we got there, the river was dry. Industries dumped their waste into the river. Big trucks passed by, and the air smelled of sewage.

"Are you sure we're in the right place?" Tara asked.

I showed her the map that was supposed to take us to the biking trail.

"But this map is old," she said.

It was a hot and humid day and our eyes burned from sweat. We stopped several times to buy water.

"Well, this is fun," she said.

"Don't be sarcastic. I am sorry."

"I am not being sarcastic," she said. "We'll find it. If there is anything to be found."

"I said I'm sorry."

When we got to the trail, we saw kids dipping their feet in the murky water. Women washed clothes on boulders. Foam floated on the surface of the stagnant water.

It wasn't what I had imagined.

On the way back to the hotel, Tara biked through a yellow traffic light. I had to stop when the light turned red. I watched her as she rode away. She didn't look back to see if I was following her.

When I got to our hotel room, the sun was setting and she wasn't there yet.

"Where did you go?" I asked when she came back, an hour later.

"I got lost," she said. "I am sorry, B. I know you're trying."

She ran her fingers through my hair.

From My Notes

The fishermen were thirsty and he didn't have any water to drink himself.

We can't breathe, they said.

The moon tasted like mercury and they all dived in deep and sipped on it.

What is the colour of your wind? they asked.

He could see colours but when he tried to name them, he remembered that he wasn't able to speak.

He swam through the leaves and rose toward the light but still couldn't breathe.

His fingernails were claws and he couldn't rip the wind off himself.

"Who're these fishermen?" the Interrogator asked. "They've been in your notes multiple times."

"Maybe you're finally trying to free yourself from the memories of your father by inventing something new."

"There'll be possibilities for you that way."

"You may be able to find a job — even be able to write."

"I've noticed you do have a knack for it."

"There may even be possibilities with your wife again."

• • •

When I opened my eyes in the darkness, the body of my writer friend was hanging from the ceiling of the c-can. His head bloated. His eyes closed.

He was whispering in another dialect.

"You shouldn't have written it," he said.

The c-can was dark and I could no longer see his face.

I tried to untie the noose, but I wasn't tall enough to reach.

The lights in the c-can blinked. The man with the deflated face took my hand and asked me to follow him. We swam toward the island, the reeds tangling my feet, the water dark.

"You need to help us," he said.

"I want to run away," I said. "I wish I could help. But I can't even swim."

But we were all on the island after. They were surrounding me. Whispering things in my ear. Fishermen. Men from the rig.

"But I don't even understand you."

"Do you want us all dead like him?" they said, pointing at my friend's body, hanging from a tree. "How can you do nothing for us?"

"I was trying to."

A pearl hunter brought in a pearl necklace and hung it from my neck.

"You're dead. All of you. I can't save anyone," I sobbed.

The pearls blinked under the sunlight. Then I was staring at the lamp in the c-can.

A guard shook me. Another one was standing with a syringe in his hand.

My eyes were wet.

• • •

I spent most of the day in the bed, drowsy and numb, my head heavy.

Days and nights muddled together.

As I gave them more pages, they let me go for a five-minute walk on the deck. I looked around at the ocean, at the little islands. I took in the humid air.

Everything seemed so far away.

The book. Tara.

A taste of ash in my mouth that wouldn't go away. Only a vague memory of the rig.

I wrote down everything I was asked to write. I signed every form that I was asked to sign.

I was there to forget and I was forgetting.

As I was forgetting, I remembered things from my childhood. Things I hadn't thought of in a long time.

From My Notes

I am a coward and conspirator like my father.

CHAPTER 6

After I'd signed all the forms they asked me to, they moved me to a cabin in the ship with two younger boys from the South.

They no longer took me to the Interrogator's office.

The cabin didn't have a window, but we could turn on the lamps ourselves. I could go to the bathroom all by myself, though they monitored the cabins and the hallways with cameras.

My eyes were getting used to being in the light again. We were permitted to take a walk around the hallway only in the morning. We weren't allowed to be on the deck by ourselves.

The bodies in white clothes fidgeted between walls, moved around in the hallways.

Necks slanted or sank into torsos. Cloudy eyes stared down at the feet. Arms twisted or stretched to other body parts. Mouths repeated the same phrase over and over.

One would repeat something until it led to a scream. Until it led to arms being pulled behind the back, the forehead pressed against the floor. The tip of a syringe under the skin. The sense of falling.

You woke up in an empty c-can again in a puddle of your piss. Your body bruised blue.

We lined up for lunch and dinner. We carried the metal trays to our tables.

We barely spoke. We heard screams in a dialect that made us think of the desert.

We lined up for pills.

Open mouth. Tongue out. Pills on tongue. Swallow.

The pills tasted like chalk.

A flash of light into the mouth made the eyes glow.

Here, they gave you a recorder.

You had to talk to your recorder every day. Give the guards your daily recordings.

On the recorder, I talked mainly about my childhood.

Hot summer days playing with my cousins in my aunt's basement. Searching in each other's underpants for what we pretended to be opium. We became gang members, smugglers passing through borders.

I made up stories, made my cousins play along.

We invented names for new places.

White sheets catching wind on the clothespins in their yard. The dust on our sweaty skins.

Those days I'd forget about my father until my aunts or uncles called us back in, until they brought up his name over a meal.

My mother sank into her chair. Her head hanging, eyes looking down at her tiny feet.

"That faggot," my uncle swore the night my mother dragged me out of their house. The cousins and I were crying.

"I didn't expect this from you," my mother said to her brother. "I didn't expect you to believe those rumours."

"For how long are you going to deny it?" my uncle said. "It doesn't matter if it's not true. He has either left you, or he's dead. You need to move on with your life."

"That's none of your business," my mother said.

My aunt started removing the plates, opening the tap to wash the dishes.

I didn't fully understand what they were talking about.

The streets were empty. My mother and I waited in the vacant bus terminal for hours.

Cars passed and honked their horns, the drivers saying things I was too young to apprehend. My mother blushed and hid me under her long scarf.

I didn't remember seeing the cousins for years after.

Whenever I asked my mother if what my uncle had said was true, she'd deny it.

"I knew your father," she said.

She said, "Leaving the state was the only way to stay alive."

She said, "All the friends he lost."

She said, "There was no other choice for him. For us."

But why had he stopped writing to us? Why didn't he send for us later?

"They would've tracked him down. Tracked us. They checked everything for a long time. They would've used us to get to him.

"He did it all for our safety."

Why hadn't we gone with him?

I believed she never found an answer to these questions. But she showed no doubt, no anger. She preferred to suppress her doubt, which frustrated me more. It left me alone with my questions.

Was he even alive? Had he ever existed?

Maybe it hadn't mattered to her as much.

Maybe she already had answers. Maybe she knew something she never told me.

All these years, she had continued to live with his memory.

"He was not like my brothers. He was very sensitive. He wanted something better for everyone. He loved us."

I'd tried to find him when I was in my early twenties. I talked to all his friends my mother knew. Friends of those friends who had known him.

Some of those friends had disappeared or been executed themselves.

One of my father's friends said he'd seen my father driving a cab several years ago at the airport of a foreign city. But my father — the man was quite sure it had been him — had denied knowing him, had denied being the person he was suggesting him to be.

I'd thought of going to that airport, to search for him at the same taxi rank. Maybe he'd recognize me.

But I didn't know who I was looking for. I didn't know what he'd changed his name to.

It was only after my mother passed away that I dared to start writing the book.

I was feeling even lonelier.

I went back to the same friends of my father whom I had talked to several years before, but some of them were dead by that time.

I talked to the colleagues, those who were alive. I didn't think about going to the city the friend had mentioned. It was too late. Even if my father wasn't dead, there was no way for me to find him.

· · ·

The limp in my leg had become permanent. I still couldn't turn my hand into a fist.

They'd let me keep the red notebook. I reread it several times, thinking about my father. I had read it while writing the book, but this time I read it differently, trying to know him through what he'd dreamed, imagining his possible futures without us.

In one he lived alone in a pine wood, wrote poetry in another language.

In another men who looked like my guards were waiting for him to return to his motel room in a foreign city. They pulled a black plastic bag over his head. His limbs jerked until he was unconscious.

In one they found him before he managed to cross the border.

Did they make him write a letter to us or forge his handwriting? I hadn't considered this before. The letter had no return address on it, which made sense as he didn't want to be traced. There was no mention of where he was sending the letter from. It had been my mother's assumption that the letter was sent from another country. I should've tried to trace where the remote-control car had come from. This hadn't occurred to me before, and it was likely too late now.

I wondered if I would ever go back home myself. Would I be able to find everything as I had left it stored in our garage?

I tried not to record anything about my father, but I got lost in my thoughts sometimes and forgot that, and then wasn't able to delete what I had recorded.

I tried to not say anything about what happened on the rig, either. I thought I had a better chance of being let go this way.

Saying more could put someone else at risk.

I pictured Tara moving around our house. Watering the apple orchard in the front yard.

I wondered if the scanned letter from her had been real, if she had really started a new life.

Maybe she had rearranged the furniture now. Packed up more of my stuff and put it in the garage.

From My Father's Notebook

The streets were dark. There was a stench in the air. The heads had turned into skinned bowls of flesh.

People lined up behind big pots of soup. A man in a respirator ladled out the soup into their skulls. They could only hold it there and couldn't eat it since they didn't have mouths.

The soup would remain in their heads until it rotted.

I lined up behind others with a bowl in my hands, then started touching my face.

I didn't have lips.

One day I saw the muscular girl who had kissed me on the rig, the girl who had asked me for help with her lighter. She was in the hallway. They'd shaved her hair and eyebrows. Her face was white like paper. She no longer had a piercing in her nose. From the window in the hallway, she stared at an unknown point in the ocean.

Her sharp cheekbones made me think of the mountains.

I became conscious of all that had happened since my arrival at the rig.

The walls of the hallway felt closer. I held my head in my hands before I lost my balance and fell onto the floor. An intense pressure behind my eyes.

When I raised my head, I noticed a guard's shadow appear from the other end of the hallway. The others scattered to their rooms.

The guard was standing by my side, looking down at me, but the girl was no longer there.

From My Father's Notebook

The birds are migrating in the sky. First there are only gulls. Then there are more birds. Geese. Storks. Pelicans made of paper. People are on the streets. It's a carnival. When I pass by you and the man, you pretend we don't know each other.

Paper birds turn into ash. It is snowing and the snow covers everything.

I follow your footprints in the snow.

Despite what had happened, they didn't take me to a c-can again. I remained in the same room with the two boys. I was still permitted to walk in the hallway in the mornings and I kept waiting to see the girl with the shaved head again, the girl with the lighter.

I looked around during the meals or as I was lining up to get my pills. But there was no sign of her anywhere.

At the end of the hallway, there was a door that was always locked, though I had seen guards entering the hallway through it. I assumed it was connected to the part of the ship where the Interrogator's office was.

I kept doubting myself. Maybe I'd made a mistake about seeing the girl who had kissed me on the rig. Maybe I had made this up, like other things I had imagined or seen in my visions.

Every day there were more holes in my memory.

I couldn't tolerate the ongoing screams in the hallway. I'd run to my room, crawl under the bedsheets, yet I'd still hear screaming.

When I hid myself, my roommate with the short torso sat by my bed and watched me like a worried dog whose owner was dying.

His spittle drooled on my bed. He kept screaming a name I didn't recognize.

I didn't want him around. But he inched forward, his hand almost touching my face. I slapped it away.

I hid my ears under the pillow on my bed.

I wanted to dig a hole and sink down into it.

•   •   •

It was only to take a shower that we'd be let on the deck. The shower area consisted of two c-cans attached together on the deck. The metal roofs had been removed. The shower stalls were separated by opaque nylon curtains.

In the shower, we had less than a minute to wash up. You'd fill a bucket with water and the guard would pull a rope that drained the cold water in the bucket on top of your head. The soap had a strong smell like the cheap soap that my mother used to buy when I was a kid.

You could see the blue sky. The clouds changing shape in the wind. Mosquitoes and flies bit you as you tried to wash yourself.

The water had a bitter taste to it.

My skin smelled of algae and soap afterward.

The entry to the shower area was covered and served as a changing room. Guards usually guided three of us into the room and watched us undress. They inspected our skin for bedbugs, our hair for lice.

There was only one woman with me in the changing room that day. Her left arm was missing. She had a moon sliver carved into her flesh near the stump.

She wasn't much older than me. Her breasts were the size of limes.

She pointed to my penis with her right hand and grinned.

"Ice cream." She laughed, holding something imaginary to her mouth, licking her lips.

I hid my penis with my hands. My spine curled down.

When the guard raised his baton over the woman's shoulders, the woman ducked.

I left the two of them there, entered my stall, rubbing soap on my skin. After I finished soaping up in my stall, I

waited for a while to rinse myself, but the guard didn't pull
the rope.

When nothing happened, I pulled the shower curtain and
looked around.

The guard wasn't there. I could hear the woman screaming
from her stall.

I left the shower with foam all over my body. I dried myself
with a towel and quickly put on my clothes. I looked around
again, but no one was there.

I thought about trying to locate the c-can I had been in
first, but I changed my mind. I walked to the main building,
dragging my bad foot on the deck until I got to the hallway.
I waited until the guard standing there turned away, then I
tiptoed toward the door at the end of the hallway. I turned
the knob and the door opened to a stairwell. From outside I
had seen rooms on the second floor. The curtains were always
drawn. I'd never been on the second floor myself, probably
other than when they'd taken me to visit my interrogator.

I climbed the stairs. There was another hallway, a replica of
the one on the first floor. Old yellowed maps covered the walls
with points pinned on them. The tallowy paint on the walls
was peeling off.

Unlike the first floor, the second floor hadn't been
renovated.

Blood rushed into my chest. I wondered which was the
Interrogator's cabin. I tried different cabin doors but the first
two doors didn't open. The third door felt flimsier. I knocked
against it with my right shoulder, using the weight of my whole
body.

The door opened and made a loud noise as it hit the wall
behind it.

I maintained my balance and didn't fall, but my knees shook from pain. I had to sit down. I looked outside to see if there was anyone in the hallway, then closed the door.

The cabin was filled with file cabinets. I crawled toward one and opened it, shoved two folders into my pants.

I stood up, closed the door and hobbled back down the stairs to the main hallway. I slowed down my steps, moving toward my own cabin as if nothing had happened.

"Hey," the guard in the hallway shouted. "What're you doing there?"

I made eye contact with him.

"The other guard disappeared," I said. "I had to clean myself up without water. Can I shower again? I am still dirty."

"Go back to your cabin," the guard said.

In the cabin, I lay under my bedsheets and took the folders out. I hid them under my pillow. I was waiting for my roommates to go to sleep before I looked at them.

"I am the dusk of the morning. I am reborn from my ashes —" the boy with the thick glasses recited. Behind his glasses, he had blue eyes.

Usually, he made elaborate origamis of birds, displayed them by his bedside.

Nobody had seen many of those birds in years.

The origamis were so detailed you could distinguish a cormorant from a pelican or a stork.

I wondered where he got the paper.

The day before, he had got frustrated and shredded the last bird he'd made.

I wondered if it had been a phoenix.

Now he was reciting a poem he'd remembered or had just made up.

The other boy, the one with the short torso, had taken off his underpants and was rubbing himself against his pillow. He grunted, then pushed the pillow against the wall and thumped at it with closed fists.

"I am the phoenix," the first boy sang. He opened his arms as if they were wings.

I kept the sheets over my chin, but didn't close my eyes. I smelled my sweat in the dampness of the cotton.

"Will the two of you keep it down?" I asked. "I am trying to sleep."

The boy in bed was now licking the corner of his pillow.

They sometimes reminded me of two boys at my kindergarten. They'd been the only kids who wanted to play with me, but I hadn't let them.

I'd be happy when they'd piss their pants and be taken to the infants' room and made to wear a diaper.

I'd be happy to be left in the yard to play alone.

I'd touch millipedes, watch them coil up into little balls.

I'd move a snail from one leaf to another. I'd taste the soil and the bark of the trees and fill with an unknown pleasure. Or at least this was how I remembered it.

I didn't remember if my father had been around at that time.

• • •

When they were both asleep, I took the folders out and tried to read the pages in the dim light. Both folders had passport-sized photos of a man on the first page. The light wasn't strong enough to read the text or make out the faces.

I hid the folders under the pillow again and tried to go back to sleep.

My bed smelled of the soap that I'd towelled off my body.

The first boy jerked in his sleep as if he was falling off a cliff in his dream.

When I woke, I was still tired. Both of the boys were up. The singing one was now sitting on the toilet seat, swaying his torso back and forth, slapping his thighs with his palms. He moved like a fisherman's wife mourning the loss of a husband to a storm.

"What's wrong?" I asked, but he didn't respond.

"Your birds are really exquisite," I said. "Did you used to be an artist?"

He turned his head this time, but he still didn't say anything.

"Or were you an ornithologist?" I asked, louder this time.

He looked around and pulled his pants up to his knees, then moved around the room with small steps, dragging his feet on the floor.

I remembered the features of his face.

"I interviewed you before, didn't I?" I asked. "About the painted storks?"

"Don't tell," he said.

It hadn't been that long ago that I had interviewed him. Did his being here have something to do with me?

He walked to the wall, put his right ear against it.

"Here," he said. "They're here again."

He pulled his pants up to his belly.

"They've come from the sea," he said.

I wondered if he was talking about the fishermen or the bad spirits.

• • •

I'd taken a pen from the file room. On a piece of toilet paper, I wrote:

> *I don't know if you remember me, but I woke up thinking of you today. I am not sure if you're even here or not.*
>   *Your cheekbones remind me of the mountains.*

I crossed out the last line, crumpled the napkin and put it in my pocket. I went to the hallway, but nobody was there yet.

Outside, the sun was rising. The sky was the colour of a peeled grapefruit.

The ship was very close to an island. At a distance, I could see a cane marsh, the rusted remnants of an old, sunken ship near the shore. Coral cliffs protruded out of the crimson sea.

This looked like the island I had seen in my visions, where the fishermen were waiting.

Since they had moved me to the cabins, the visions had become less frequent.

I was a bit more attuned to my surroundings, despite the gaps in my memory and the pills they still made me take.

I heard dogs barking on the island.

A dumpster with old boats, scavenged metals piled up on top of each other, glinted in the morning light.

It was on the same day at lunchtime that I saw the girl from the rig again, sitting several tables away from me. She was sitting alone, her head shaved, her brown eyes looking down at her plate. I had not been mistaken about seeing her the first time.

When she looked up, her face didn't change, but she took her plate and came to our table, sat there with her food.

I didn't dare say anything.

We continued eating.

. . .

In the folders, there were pages about two men, one of them a labour activist, the other a lawyer.

I didn't recognize their names.

There weren't any dates on the documents. Every page was stamped as classified. There was information about where the two men worked and lived. The addresses of their houses, the workplaces of their spouses. Schools their children attended.

In the case of the lawyer, there was information about a woman he'd had an affair with.

Her address. The name of her husband.

The lawyer had been involved in a case against the Company in which fifty-seven workers were dead from chemical poisoning.

There were transcripts of interactions between the lawyer and the woman he had had the affair with.

The pages of the folders were dusty. The folders shook in my hands and fell to the floor. Perhaps there were similar files on other people from other periods.

I picked up the folders again. I shredded the pages into small pieces and flushed them down the toilet. This was how they'd always operated, trying to find dirt on you to keep you muzzled, generating it when they couldn't find anything.

I kept only one page, crossed out everything that was on it.
On the back of it I wrote:

> *The third time I saw you, your eyebrows had*
> *grown again. This time we weren't lining up.*
> *We were sitting quietly, spooning the mushy*
> *soup into our mouths.*
>
> *This was all they fed us. Parsnip soup. Boiled*
> *potatoes. We had only a spoon to eat with, had*
> *to peel and puree the potato with our hands. We*
> *were always thirsty.*
>
> *When you came to my table and sat with*
> *me, we didn't even greet each other. We didn't*
> *even dare raise our heads, never mind talk.*
>
> *How I wished we'd met somewhere else.*
>
> *You never again looked like the first night*
> *I saw you. They'd taken something away from*
> *you. From us.*
>
> *I had the napkin with the note in my pocket*
> *but didn't dare give it to you.*
>
> *I haven't seen our friend, the Assistant Cook,*
> *since he disappeared on the rig. Do you know*
> *what happened to him? Is he here with us?*

I read it again, shredded what I'd written. I wrote another
note instead:

> *I don't know what happened to our friend. I*
> *haven't seen him since that man lit himself on*
> *fire.*

The next day at lunch, she sat with me again. I looked around and, when the guard wasn't looking at us, I passed the napkin to her.

Our hands touched slightly. I was surprised by how cold hers were.

• • •

A cold fall day hiking in the mountains with Tara. She'd handed me a letter. I couldn't remember what the letter was about.

I remembered that as soon as I got home that night, I called her. We talked until dusk.

I missed those days. The cold mountain air. Our long walks. Her voice on the phone.

We'd been so happy at the beginning. Things had started to change after. I didn't get that many freelance assignments and started driving a truck to compensate for it. So many days away from home. Tara spent more time at her job and with her parents even when I was there.

"You hardly say a word these days," she'd say.

The owner of the shipping company was a petty thief who used any opportunity to belittle me. After I paid for the truck, gas, and his share, there was little money left.

I had no time to write. I made a habit of stopping the truck whenever I could, to make notes for my future writings.

But when I went back to my notes, they didn't make much sense.

That day I was delivering a package on a rural road. I'd been driving for days through the snow. I pulled over and slept in the truck when I got too tired. From the hours of sitting, I'd bleed every time I had a bowel movement.

I remembered the dim, cold toilets in gas stations. Sitting on the toilet seat and straining. The toilet paper red with blood. Other truck drivers lined up behind the door.

They rubbed their hands together, eyeing me suspiciously as I exited. Steam came out of their mouths.

I'd buy a bag of ice from every gas station, place it under me. I'd replace the bag at my next stop.

Tara had told me several times to stop working for the thief. She'd been stable at her position for two years then.

When I decided to leave the job, I called Tara from a gas station. I was going to sell the truck. I was going to write more.

But maybe it was already too late.

Maybe I'd already lost the battle.

We sold the truck two days later. Several days after, Tara drove me to a job interview for an office job. The streets were crowded with people rushing to get to work. Mothers were taking kids to school.

"Why do the kids have to wake up so early?" I asked.

I felt sad for all the kids who had to grow up.

"Why would anybody want to have children?" I said, my voice trembling.

Tara looked at me and pressed her hand on mine. She pulled over.

"Let's get a tea first," she said.

"You'll be late for work," I replied.

"There's time."

•   •   •

Here, I rarely had to talk other than to my recorder. I talked about being a quiet teenager.

My mother would beg me to talk to my uncles and aunts, to my cousins.

We'd reunited after several years, but the closeness was no longer there.

I'd stutter single words. I'd talk so quietly that no one would even hear me. My words would be erased as soon as they left me.

"You can't even buy underwear for a girlfriend," my uncle said once. "How're you going to get married?"

I was only seventeen. I didn't plan to marry. But this was not about getting married.

"He's like his father," I imagined him saying to my mother. "He has big illusions."

I imagined others thinking or saying the same things. Neighbours. Tara's parents.

And maybe they were all right. This was where my illusions had led me, despite me trying to prove others wrong.

● ● ●

The next day in the hallway, I watched the islands appear through the morning fog. We'd never been so close to an island. My eyes searched the cane marshes for birds, wishing I had binoculars.

I could hear the barking of dogs. The sound of crickets.

I could see big banyan trees on the island; but no boats or fishermen. It looked like a deserted island from where we were, not so dissimilar to the one in my visions.

That day she didn't sit with me during lunch. I realized they might have found my note. They might have asked her not to sit with me.

We'd lost our ritual.

Maybe I'd asked for too much. I tried to meet her eyes, but she didn't even turn to meet my gaze.

From My Father's Notebook

I am riding my bicycle in the alleys around my childhood house. My mother is alive.

The yard is covered with rotten leaves. I rake them and pile them up in a corner.

But there are more and more.

Inside the house, my mother has stained the bedsheets. I change the sheets and give her a bath. She holds my hand and spins lightly around the room, dancing.

She is young again.

After lunch that day, they took me to the Interrogator's office.
They hadn't taken me there in a long time.

When I sat, he wiggled his finger at the guard to leave the
cabin.

I felt cold in his air-conditioned cabin.

"Good to see you again," he said.

He kept the pen between his peace fingers, stared at a point
on his lap.

The air conditioner hummed.

"What's been happening?" he finally asked, breaking the
silence.

"Not much."

"And how've you been?" The corner of his lips curled, a little
bubble forming on his lower left lip.

I stared at the red tie he was wearing under his coat.

"The same," I said.

He uncrossed his legs, flipped through the pages, looking
at his notes.

"So, no specific reason for your recent behaviour?"

"What behaviour?" I asked.

He waited again, his face expressionless as usual.

"I was happy to see that you're making progress. We were so
close to letting you go back to your normal life. But you seem
to have relapsed into your past habits. You're resisting again.

"My staff say you have been leaving strange notes around.
It is making others uncomfortable. Don't you want to go back
to your life?"

I sank deeper into the chair.

"I've considered trying a different approach," he said.

He took out some photos from inside an envelope and
spread them on the table between us.

The first photo was of me, my cousin, and my father in the foothills of a mountain.

My father had turned over a stone and was showing us the insects underneath it. We were looking at the insects.

In the photo, my father looked younger than I was now. I remembered I hadn't seen myself in a mirror for a long time.

In the next photo, the three of us were running and jumping down a grassy hill. It must've been an early fall day. I hadn't seen these photos before.

I expected the Interrogator to ask questions about these or about my father.

But he covered the photos with another photo. This one had been taken from a close distance, of the back of a woman.

I recognized the yellowed sheets. A hand was pressing the head into the mattress. The back of the neck was bruised.

"Do you want to tell me about this?" the Interrogator asked.

I looked away from the photos. My knees shook.

I tried to stand up by holding onto the chair's arm, but I couldn't maintain my balance.

"I think it was something planned from before. It couldn't have been just a random encounter between me and her," I said. "I assumed she was working for you, but why would you hurt her?"

"I could ask you the same question, no?" the Interrogator said. "Everything is relative." He smiled. "Would you want to be on trial as a murderer? You've confessed yourself that you don't remember what happened after.

"What if something more serious happened to her after? What if we make it seem like you did it?" he said. "Because apparently all the things you wrote down and signed before didn't mean anything to you.

"Because we value honesty beyond anything else.

"Because we are only getting closer when you run away from us.

"As you can see, there is not only you who can be affected — there are others. People who may be important or unimportant to you.

"Guard," the Interrogator shouted.

I saw him coming closer, then he was standing above me.

"She is fine for now," he said. "She is a valuable asset, so our preference is to keep her alive."

I didn't know what I was thinking, but I kicked him with my good leg, tried to stand up again, leaning on my arms.

The door opened and more guards came in. They gathered around me, held me down as I screamed and grabbed at the air.

The Interrogator came closer and gave me an injection.

•   •   •

We were a caravan walking through the desert.

The fishermen walked in front, carrying a tray of dead fish on their heads.

Tara and you were both wearing bridal dresses.

Your hair had grown back. I looked at Tara, looking at her for permission before kissing you.

When I looked back, I didn't recognize the rest of the crowd.

At the back of the caravan, three horses pulled three corpses across the sand.

The bodies had left a long red trail behind us in the desert. I didn't know who the bodies belonged to.

I was thirsty. The wind blew the sand over the horses.

The horses neighed, kicked their heels in the air, and stopped moving.

The crows cawed and covered the sky like a black velvet curtain.

Tara disappeared.

The Interrogator draped me and you under a bedsheet. We started undressing.

CHAPTER 7

I opened my eyes in darkness, hugging my knees on the floor. My jaw hurt from clenching my teeth. I was wet and cold.

The girl with the lighter was kneeling by my side, splashing water on my face from a pail.

"Wake up," she said.

She put her hand on my forehead as if checking my temperature. I felt the coldness of her hands. Her soft skin.

I pushed her hand away. Tears had dried in the corners of my eyes. My eyelashes stuck together.

I spat blood onto the floor.

"Breathe," she said. "We have to leave fast. We don't have much time left. The ship is going to move again."

The c-can smelled of urine.

The door was wide open. How had she even gotten into my c-can?

The lamp and the surveillance camera were off. She lit a lantern with a match. My eyes followed our long shadows on the metal walls.

My rib cage hurt when I inhaled.

The smell of kerosene mixed with the smell of urine. I could see the soft hair regrown on her head in the dim light.

I rolled on the floor with the pain I had become aware of again.

I remembered the guards kicking me. The Interrogator had given me an injection.

"You've got to trust me on this one. We'll have to swim to the island. We may find locals who can help us there."

I remembered the voices calling me in different dialects. The light of their lanterns flickered at the darkness of the night. I was standing on a cliff, talking to them. We were going to join together. The fishermen, the prisoners, the roughnecks.

"The fishermen?" I asked.

"I am just trying to help you get out of here. I don't know what you're talking about."

"I've been having this vision —"

"Listen, I'm not sure what you're talking about. I know things may be fuzzy now, but we need to leave. You need to follow me."

She was wearing boots and a wetsuit like the ones the guards wore when washing me with a hose. It alarmed me after all I had been through. What if she was another state agent, like the tall woman from the bookstore?

"But won't they find us?" I said. "Can't they hurt others? They threatened to kill that woman."

"Look, things are only going to get worse here. That's all I can tell you. Some of the things they say are just threats."

She had a black garbage bag that rustled when she moved.

"So, you are not with them?" I asked.

"We don't have time for this now. I'll tell you more when we're safe."

I decided to follow her. I didn't want to be stuck in the c-can or the cabin again.

She handed me a life jacket to wear. It was covered with black tape so as not to attract attention from a distance.

"How about you?"

"We only have one. I'll be fine without it," she said. "I am a great swimmer." She smiled.

She pulled out the map from the garbage bag, looked at it under the lantern light, then folded it and put it back in her jacket pocket.

She handed me a letter inside an envelope, then blew on the lantern.

I could see her eyes and lips in the light before the lantern sputtered and the light was gone.

"This explains everything. But I want you to read it when you're alone, when we're safe."

She sat on her knees, wrapped my right arm around her shoulders, then stood to lift me. I pushed my right foot against the floor, leaning on her.

Her body felt strong against mine.

I became dizzy as I stood and leaned on the wall, which was still warm.

She took a sugar packet out of the pocket of her jacket, asked me to open my mouth. She emptied the packet into my mouth.

She pushed some more packets of sugar into the pocket of my life jacket.

"Take more when your blood sugar drops," she whispered. She gave me one end of a rope to hold. "Wait for me here. I'll let you know when to follow by pulling the rope."

I held the rope loose in my hand and waited, hearing rustling and creaking in the darkness. When the rope became alive in my hands, I followed it through the c-cans, tiptoeing and looking around.

The sky was cloudy and the lights in the ship were off. I couldn't see much.

When I got to the edge of the deck, I heard the sound of her breathing and the wind hitting against the c-cans.

In the darkness, my eyes detected the borders of her body. She was kneeling. A rope ladder hung from the deck, the other end of the ladder swaying in the water.

She asked me to go first. As I was climbing down the ladder, I heard the waves loud against the ship. The water was pitch black.

I leaped into the wavy, cold water, holding onto the ladder, trying to not make any noise. I waited for her to climb down, holding onto the end of the ladder.

When she was in the water, I wrapped my arms around her. She was no longer wearing the rain jacket.

"Isn't it better if you wear the life jacket?" I whispered.

I wondered what she had done with the garbage bag as she no longer had anything with her.

As she swam, the waves moved us up and down. A blue neon light glowed from millions of plankton. The waves moved the colourful dots around our bodies.

My shoulders hurt. Numbness spread to my fingers. My back tingled.

"Hold me," she said.

"Can you see the island?" I shouted.

She kept swimming. Maybe she hadn't heard me.

Then it started to rain. First it was only small drops, but it soon changed to a shower pouring onto us.

I couldn't see much around me.

Her short hair was soaked. The back of her neck.

I didn't even know her name.

"What's your name?" I shouted. This time she said something, but I didn't hear her.

The waves rose higher. Salty water got into my nostrils and throat.

I coughed, then let go of her as I was making it harder for her to swim.

I tried to swim, but had little strength left.

I saw her swimming toward me. I stroked the water, but the waves swept me around.

I felt tiny against the wind and water.

• • •

The sea was calm again. I couldn't spot her, but could see the cane marsh and the coral reefs of the island through the morning haze. I looked back but I couldn't see the cargo ship or the old sunken ship.

I was floating on the water.

All my joints ached.

I wondered if I was near the same island, or the waves had taken me somewhere else.

I remembered the letter in the pocket of my life jacket, all the ink probably washed out. The paper turned into a pulpy paste.

I took out a packet of sugar and licked.
Had she managed to swim to the island before me?
I started swimming toward the east.

CHAPTER 8

The clouds were like blood-soaked cotton balls. Fishing boats floated at a distance.

The gulls gathered around the boats. Men on decks pulled up nets.

"Help," I screamed and heard my own voice echo through the coral cliffs.

I heard the roaring of a motor, and two fishermen rode closer on their boat. They didn't look like the men in my dream.

The younger man stretched a paddle toward me. But as I was trying to grab it, the older man screamed at him.

The younger man pulled the paddle away.

The older man started the motor again and the boat motored away.

"Help," I screamed. "Please don't go!"

I floated on my back and closed my eyes.

Maybe because I wasn't a local, they didn't want to help me.

Maybe they knew something about the cargo ship.

• • •

In the distance, I could see clay houses. The water was shallow. I waded through the marsh, with the reeds tangling my feet. When I got closer to the shore, I walked carefully so as not to slip on the moss-covered rocks.

On the shore, I lay down on the sand and had the last sugar packet.

I was thirsty.

I looked around for any sign of her.

I could walk to the village, but I didn't have any money to buy food or water from the locals. But maybe some of them would help me. Or I could tell them that I'd pay them back when I got to the city or got in touch with Tara, though it was possible that they'd tapped Tara's phone. That they would find me if I contacted her. I was hopeful that I could find the girl and she would have better ideas than mine.

I took off the life jacket after taking the letter out of its pocket. The paper hadn't fully disintegrated.

My bare feet touched the hot sand. I walked in the direction of the palm trees and the clay houses.

The air was hot, like when you open an oven door. The sweating and heat started again. Flies and mosquitoes buzzed in my ears. I looked back at my footprints that remained on the sand.

I wondered if I should knock at the village doors when I got there, but I was afraid that with my shabby appearance, nobody would let me in.

My shirt was soaked and dirty. I had taken off my pants so I could swim more easily. I had only underwear on.

Maybe I'd have a better shot at night. I could bear the hunger, but to survive until night, I'd need fresh water.

I walked in the direction of the houses. The sun was low in the sky and I felt the heat on my skin. The houses seemed close at first, but after I'd walked a long time, still they were at the same distance. When I looked back at the ocean, I could better see my progress and decided to continue.

In the main square of the village, there was a well with a pump. The pump was broken, but there was a pulley and pail to draw water with. I threw the pail into the well and pulled. I dipped my head into the pail to cool down and drank from it.

The water was lukewarm and bitter, but I was so thirsty.

I wiped my mouth and beard. I threw the pail back into the well and sat there. I looked around, then pulled the letter out to read. I was about to open it when somebody screamed behind me.

"Possessed," a girl was screaming.

She was barefoot, wearing a long white cotton dress that reached to her ankles.

"No, no," I said. "I am not from here. I was just drinking water."

She was trying to say something, but she only stuttered.

Men came out of their houses, a couple of them carrying pipes and machetes. They circled around me, swinging their machetes in the air.

I was holding the letter in my fist.

At first I thought they'd taken me to be mad or possessed,
but they seemed to have another concern.

"You have to pay us for the water," an older man said, who'd
shown up after the others and could speak perfectly in our dialect. He was probably the headman of the village.

"I'm not from around here. I don't have any money on me,
but I can probably pay you if I can make a phone call."

The girl's body convulsed like an epileptic. Her eyelids flut-
tered and I could see only the whites of her eyes. Two women
lifted her head and held her by her shoulders, splashing her face
with water. Biting their lips and chanting.

"Give me the phone number and I'll call it," the older man
said.

We waited there until a boy brought us pen and paper. I
wrote my name and Tara's name and her number.

"Follow these guys to the hut," he said.

The men didn't drag me like the guards did. They let me
walk myself, and slowed down their steps to my speed. They
stared at my bare legs, which were bruised and covered in sand.

They opened the hut, guided me in, and shut the door.

The hut smelled of manure and hay. Through the cracks, I
could see bodies moving outside.

Sweat kept rolling down from my armpits. My skin itched
from the insect bites. My muscles still hurt from the kicking
of the guards.

I leaned on the door and didn't move.

• • •

In the light through the cracks, the first several lines of the
letter were readable.

*I'm sorry that I didn't try to help you earlier. I
don't know how to explain this. I hope when you
read this, you'll be able to understand. I was just
an informant on the rig who was supposed to get
close to you, but the plans changed after. Then
they brought me here to get close to you again.*

*I think you were on their radar before be-
cause of your father, and your collaboration
with the Editor alarmed them even more.*

The next sentences had all blended together and weren't
easy to read. The only words I could distinguish were:

Rig.
Father.

Then, at the end of the letter, I could read:

I AM SORRY.

It had been written in a larger font.

I wondered if she would know something more about my
father. I wondered if the Assistant Cook had also been an informant, but there was no way for me to know.

• • •

The next time they came into the hut, a young man tied my
hands. He brought a bowl of water up to my face.

I drank it like a thirsty animal, the water dribbling down
my beard.

"Slow down," he said. "You'll choke yourself."

"Phone," I said. "My wife. Did you call her?"

"Nobody responded," he said. He sniffed the air. "Do you have to go to the toilet again?"

He opened the door and held the rope loosely, letting me walk in front of him.

The sun was clammy in the sky. A thin old goat was tied to a rod near the well.

Two women in colourful dresses were sitting there, grinding black seeds in a stone bowl. Their hair was braided and their dresses clung to their bodies with their sweat. They raised their heads and looked at us, sweat dripping from their foreheads.

"Knock on the wall the next time you need to go. It stinks in there."

"I am hungry," I said. "Can you give me something to eat?"

"You have to wait a little. Father has pitied you, or maybe he has seen something in you. He wants to help you. But you have to fast before the ceremony."

"Is your father a fisherman?"

"We're mostly fishermen here, but some of us are farmers."

"What will they do to me after?"

"He might just let you go, drop you off at the port after you've healed. Or ask you to stay and work in the palm yards to pay your debt. He may ask you to marry the girl, because nobody else will marry her now."

I tried to remember the girl in the white dress, but I couldn't.

"But I am married," I said.

Several vultures circled in the blue sky. If they just left me here with nothing, I'd die from thirst.

I only needed to wait for tonight and they'd let me go, though I didn't know what I was going back to.

The air smelled of charcoal. I could see smoke in the distance.

I'd seen a sacrifice ceremony before.

These people were so short on food. I didn't understand why they were going to make a sacrifice for me.

The goat was grazing on the dry hay in front of it, not knowing its fate.

The boy took me back to the hut and locked the door.

• • •

I looked at the letter again, trying to see if I could understand anything more from it, but I could only make out the same words.

I wondered why Tara hadn't responded to the phone call. I hoped she was safe. Had she moved out of the house?

I imagined going back home. Opening the door to our house, seeing her in the kitchen.

I fidgeted around the hut. I couldn't tolerate the hunger anymore. I filled my mouth with dried hay. It scratched my throat as it went down.

Pain clawed my abdomen. The man with the deflated face knocked on the walls, trying to find his way out.

"Come on, open the door," we shouted.

The walls swelled and bulged. My body convulsed in the heat.

The sound of reeds and drums. The fishermen rubbed my forehead with their soot-covered hands.

I knocked on the walls.

"I'll save all of you," I said. "Please let me go."

They kneeled by my feet, holding onto my ankles. I was drowning in a black liquid.

"Beware of the wind" repeated in my head.

• • •

The door was open. I could see them dancing by the fire. I was stretched on the ground and my skin was covered with a herbal poultice. It had a strong smell.

The local girl who had thought I was possessed was lying on the ground several metres away from me. They rubbed a wet cloth over our skins, then threw a white shroud over my head and carried me on their shoulders.

I didn't resist.

I saw a red glow through the white shroud, shadows moving in the dark to the sound of drums and reeds.

The man pulled the shroud off my face and held the goat down, kneeling on his knees. He pushed the goat's head toward the ground before he beheaded it with his machete.

He rubbed his fingers on the goat's neck, then rubbed my face with the blood.

The decapitated head made a noise like a chugging faucet.

I pictured the bloated head of my writer friend.

I inhaled smoke from platters moving in the air.

I raised my head and saw the stars.

The sweet taste of the dates in my mouth.

The smell of rosewater, of wild rue.

"Leave us," the man shouted.

The girl was dancing to the music. Women stood around her in white dresses.

The waves moved the luminescent plankton around. The storks opened their wings.

I saw my own face in the stars, contorting to look like my father's.

Tara's fingertips stroked my cheeks.

The shroud was back over my head, stained with the goat's blood.

. . .

The sound of the propeller at a distance. Music stopping.

The local girl's body rigid like a wooden plank.

Dogs barked. I heard shots in the distance, then saw bullets landing at the ankles of the men.

Bodies of young men fell in the sand as they ran to the houses.

Women sobbed by a wounded body.

The old man walked into the fire.

"Leave us," he screamed, raising his hands to the sky.

The goat's head on the platter stared at me.

I heard another loud noise.

CHAPTER 9

I didn't remember much of the rest. There may have been days in between. Maybe months.

I didn't remember a place after. Just blurry scenes. Narrow, dark hallways. A body dragged across the floor.

Faceless men. All surrounded by fog.

Flashlight in the eyes. Food spooned into mouth, tubed into nostrils.

I opened my eyes in a white room afterward. Not remembering.

The room was well lit, curtains pulled open. My eyes followed the square of natural light extending, moving through the room. I couldn't follow it all the way.

The room turned dark. I slept and woke again. From the corner of my eyes, I could see shadows of bodies passing, pressing against the field of my vision.

I heard whispers. But I couldn't distinguish words, not understanding what they meant.

Were they talking in dialect, in another language?

Then a soft voice. Talking to me every day.

Her face — I didn't recognize.

The nurses changed the sheets, turned me around, cleaned my back with a washcloth.

They pierced me with needles in search of something.

They put me into a wheelchair after, took me down the hallway to another room. I heard a loud noise thumping. I screamed.

"It's over, it's done now," they said.

Most of the time I was cold.

Then a tingling in my hands. I could move my head again. Nod. But I didn't feel much below my waist.

In the room, I looked out the window. Saw trees.

Green leaves glinting in the light.

The clouds.

At first they were just abstract shapes trembling in the wind. Then I started to recognize what they were.

Took many days for the words for them to come back. They came back slowly. One by one.

It was spring and I heard birds singing.

Were there still birds?

Or was this another world? A better one.

There was a woman. She was familiar. She didn't come every day, but still talked to me when she did. I missed her soft voice the days she didn't come. I waited for her. Sometimes I cried when she talked. She caressed my head. Her hair shone in the room's light.

. . .

Later, they took me in an ambulance to a house. Was it my house?

She came with me. She didn't talk to me as much as she had in the hospital. She was very quiet. Her face looked sad.

There was a front yard with an apple tree. A walnut tree in the alley I could watch from the window.

She spooned soup into my mouth. She cut my long hair in front of the mirror as I sat in the wheelchair.

She held a mirror behind me. "It's the best I could do." She laughed. "Sorry, it's not the greatest haircut."

She then rubbed shaving foam onto my face and shaved me. She wiped my face with a warm towel.

"You look like yourself again," she said after, holding my face between her hands, looking at the mirror.

But I didn't recognize the gaunt face. The white hair.

I was feeling pain again. At first it was a sharp pain, then it dulled. The medication dulled everything, not only the pain. It was the worst when I tried to move from the wheelchair to the toilet seat. She helped me at first. She pushed the wheelchair close to the seat, kneeled and wrapped my right arm around her shoulders. I pressed up against the wheelchair's right arm. Our bodies shook under the weight. Her neck and hair damp with sweat.

As I leaned on her, I was reminded of another face. Short hair. Sharp cheekbones. I had leaned on her, too. I wondered what had happened to her.

She left me alone in the bathroom and had to come back to flush when I was done. I was embarrassed.

In the bathroom, she undressed me as I sat on a plastic chair, then removed her own pants so as not to get wet. She shampooed my hair, massaging my scalp. She rubbed me with a washcloth after — my back, my feet, between my fingers.

"Close your eyes," she said before she washed me down.

She left the house for most of the day, then came back. Worked in the kitchen while the TV was on. Chopped the vegetables. Washed the dishes. Blended the cooked vegetables to make soup. The sound of the blender was monstrous, like the noise of other machines.

At the beginning, everything tasted the same to me. She usually fed me before she ate herself. We didn't sit at the table together. She ate quickly, standing, normally forking up a salad or biting into a small sandwich.

Sometimes she turned on the TV for me when she left the house. She left it mostly on the nature channel, thinking something else might be too much for me, that it would agitate me, that anything could agitate me.

The videos were from many years ago, when there was still a wider variety of birds and fish, different wildlife. A bird made a nest for its mate. Wild dogs chased a herd of deer. They chased them for kilometres until they were in open fields where the deer couldn't hide, closed in on them until there was no chance for them to run. The strong jaws broke the flesh apart. There were vultures after. Crows. Flies. It all seemed connected. Cruel.

Other people came to see us. They smiled at me. Looked into my eyes with concern.

"Do you remember us?" they asked.

They looked familiar, but I couldn't say for sure. I tried to smile.

She didn't let them stay long or ask many questions.

"They think his memory loss is not because of the injury, but because of the emotional trauma," she explained. "They think it'll be temporary."

"He needs to rest now," she added.

Some days she drove me back to the hospital. They helped me regain my muscle strength by working with weights, giving me massages. They placed a hot towel on my body at the end. I was relearning how to use my hands.

"Can we switch his appointments to Wednesdays?" she asked the receptionist. "It would work much better with my schedule at work."

"Unfortunately, Mondays are the only time we have available for the next couple of months."

"But I called before and they said I can reschedule him, and I just need to let you know when I am here."

"I don't know who you talked to before, but I am afraid his current time is the only time we can accommodate him."

When we arrived home, she went to the bedroom and shut the door, and didn't come out for several hours.

• • •

Most days she pushed my wheelchair to a park nearby. Dogs ran around in a grass field, chasing each other. They looked happy. People talked around the field as the dogs played.

The smell of wet grass made me think of watermelons.

A kid held a dog's face in his hands and laughed.

My eyes became wet.

Once, it rained when we were at the park. "B," she said, "do you like the rain?"

Maybe she had said my name before. But I remembered my name.

The rain was wet and cool. I opened my mouth and tasted it. It didn't taste of anything.

Tiny drops of rain were in the air when the sun came out. The air looked as if it sparkled with gold.

I remembered her name.

I gained enough strength to push the wheelchair around the house myself. The skin of my hands came off as I moved around more, putting more pressure on my hands.

"I should've thought of it," Tara said. She got me gloves several days later.

Memories came back slowly. Of sad times in the house. My writing and drinking. Happy memories from a more distant past. My mother and my father.

"Tara, do you still have our early letters?" I asked her.

"They should be in the garage somewhere," she said. "Why do you ask?"

"I just thought of them — remember we ended up reading all of them each time we moved."

"We didn't do it when we moved here." She sighed. "I don't remember when we did it last." Her forehead wrinkled. She had wrapped her hair in a ponytail.

Why did we write so many letters when we saw each other every day?

Then there were the memories of the rig. The c-cans. Their darkness. The Interrogator's face. The guards.

I had nightmares. In the nightmares, I woke in the same house. But a stranger was standing beside my bed, a syringe in his hand.

I tried to scream, but I didn't have a voice.

Tara slept in another room, but she would come to my room to wake me when I screamed in my sleep.

"Easy," she said. "It's okay. We're safe here." She pressed her hand against my shoulder. "You are home, B," she said.

But I couldn't believe her. It was hard to believe anything.

· · ·

"Did you have a chance to find those letters?" I asked Tara.

"Why are you asking?" she asked. "Why do you have to do this?"

"Do what?"

"Nothing, forget it," she said. She walked to the bedroom and I followed her there. She started removing her clothes quickly and putting on different ones, not looking at me. She had just arrived home and changed.

The corner of her lip quivered.

"Where are you going?"

"Nowhere. Where can I go? I'll be back to give you your dinner."

"I'm not hungry," I said. Then I shouted, "You don't need to feed me."

She took the car keys and left the house, slamming the door behind her.

I rolled myself to the window. I took off the gloves and threw them onto the floor.

The image of another woman's face swimming in the ocean passed through my head. I was holding onto her. The waves were high. Then I let go.

. . .

My hands learned how to open the fridge again, turn on the
TV and change the channel. Soon I could hold a pen, though
my handwriting looked strange.

On the streets, there were groups of people chanting slogans. Tires burning. The terrible smoke made us cough.

"We need to go home," she said, pushing my wheelchair
faster as the guards' motorcycles showed up.

"Don't look that way," she said as if I was a child who needed to be protected.

I kept looking back, worrying someone was following us. At
home I moved my wheelchair to the window and stayed there
for many hours. The house was in an alley, but I could see a
man waiting in a car on the main street.

"Aren't you going to rest?" Tara asked.

I watched the car until the man finally left.

Some days I heard sirens, saw people running into the alley
to hide from the guards.

"Will I ever be able to walk again?" I asked her.

She had just returned from work and was putting the dirty
dishes in the dishwasher. "Yes, they think you will, but you'll
have to work a bit harder."

She left what she was doing and she came and sat on a chair
in front of me.

She started to cry.

"What is it?" I asked.

"I'm not sure I can do this anymore," she said. "And it's not
about your recovery. Because I've done everything I can.

"Something had changed, even before you left," she said. "I
guess you felt it, too."

She said, "We both tried back then."

I heard the sirens of an ambulance or a police car passing by on the main street.

"I know how hard it must be for you, but I don't think we'll be able to continue like this."

This didn't come as a surprise. Maybe I had expected it all along. Maybe my senses were so muted then that it no longer shook me. Here was something I had been afraid of, but it didn't feel like much.

"You may feel safer if you leave the country," she said. "I am worried for you here. Maybe you can start fresh somewhere else. Here you'll always be looking out for them."

"What about you?" I asked.

"I may do the same. I have considered leaving. But we each have to have our own plans."

I remembered the letter from her that the Secretary had shared with me when I was on the rig. I didn't believe that it was real. I still thought they'd forged it. I didn't ask her about it.

"The most important thing now is that you continue your rehabilitation," she said as she embraced me.

My head touched her breasts. Her body was warm.

I didn't ask her when I'd have to leave the house. I didn't ask what I would do without her.

•   •   •

I started writing things as I remembered more. On the street, the cars honked in protest. A cloud of smoke rose in the distance.

We heard explosions in the middle of the night. But no one knew what was happening.

The state TV described the events as scattered riots by the enemies of the people.

Several days later, a car was set on fire in our neighbourhood. The bank windows were broken.

One day Tara didn't return from work at her usual time. I waited impatiently, wondering what had happened. When she came back home, she said everyone was in the streets.

"I wasn't even planning to join the protest," she said. "But I was almost arrested. A guy kicked the guard who had grabbed my shirt and I was able to run."

She showed me her shirt, which was ripped.

"My eyes are burning," she said.

They had used tear gas to attack everyone who had gathered. The crowd had scattered. But many were arrested.

I remembered the day on the rig when the man had set himself on fire.

*   *   *

I wrote whatever I remembered. First I wrote with a pen. I was like someone who had just learned the alphabet. The more time I spent on writing, the clearer the events became. One memory would lead me to another.

How had they let me go? Was I no longer a threat to them?

I feared they'd come after me again, that I would be abducted. I didn't want to give them another excuse.

I started writing on a laptop, saved the file on a memory stick, and deleted everything I had written from the laptop. I put the memory stick in a plastic bag and hid it in the toilet tank. Every day after I was done with writing, I would do this.

Tara once heard the noise as I lifted the toilet tank cover and placed it on the sink. She saw me with the bag and the memory stick, but she didn't say anything. She went back to whatever she was doing.

She didn't ask me what I was writing. She didn't ask me what had happened. Maybe it wasn't too hard to imagine. Maybe she thought it would be too painful for me, or too intimate, seeing as she wanted us to go our own ways.

One day I saw the Publisher outside in our alley as I was looking out the window. He reached our door and rang the bell. I wondered what he wanted after all that had happened. I waited, watching him there in his ugly grey suit, wiping sweat from his bald head with a napkin. I didn't open the door. He kept ringing and looking around until he got tired of it and left.

"Is the book about my father still available in the bookstores?" I asked Tara when she got home that day.

"I haven't seen it in a while," she said. "I didn't know if you cared about it."

"I don't," I said. I didn't tell her anything about the Publisher showing up at our door. "What did you think of it? I don't even know what they ended up publishing."

"It didn't feel like something you would write. I stopped after a couple of pages."

"Do you have a copy of it?" I asked.

"A friend of mine borrowed it and never returned it."

"Which friend?"

"Do you know all my friends? You don't know him."

"I was just curious."

Several days later, the Publisher came back when Tara was home, and she let him in.

"How're you doing, B? I am sorry I haven't been in touch. But I thought bringing your royalty cheque would be a good opportunity to see you again."

I didn't respond and rolled the wheelchair toward the window. How could he show up here at our house after what he had done?

He helped himself to the couch.

Tara went into the kitchen and came out with a bowl of cherries and strawberries and a glass of water, placing them on the coffee table. She sat across from the Publisher in a chair.

"I know you're upset with the way things went with the book. But I was under a lot of pressure then. I didn't have much of a choice. They pushed me to publish it before I had a chance to hear back from you. But publishing it was still better than not publishing it, no?"

I remembered the first time I had seen the Interrogator. "Your book is published. You should be happy now," was one of the first things he had said to me.

When I didn't say anything, the Publisher said, "Let's agree to disagree on that. But here is your cheque." He came closer and handed it to me.

I opened the envelope and looked at it. It was a fair amount. More than I was expecting.

Given all the expenses of the hospital, I felt even more indebted to Tara. I also needed to rent a place of my own soon.

But how was there any money from the sale of a book that wasn't available at bookstores anymore?

"But how is this possible?" I asked.

"Well, B, I know how to navigate these turbulent waters and get by. I haven't been arrested once in my life and managed a reputable publishing house despite everything. As I told you before, everything is about negotiation."

I rolled closer to the couch where he was sitting, my voice shaking, heat rushing to my ears.

"You destroyed everything — you're the state's dog. That's probably how you've survived this long. I don't want to hear from you again. You can just mail the cheque next time."

He paused, then took a strawberry and placed it in his mouth, sucked on it as he looked at me.

"Let me explain myself better. Because the reality cannot be more different. Things are more porous and complicated than you think. If it is up to the state, they do not want a single book to be published. But we are always talking about a balance of different forces. That's how we do it. Why do you think you are back in the comfort of your own home? Couldn't they have kept you in some dark cell? But you had a book, people read it. Your name was known to some. We were able to negotiate."

He drank the water from the glass, waiting for a response.

"But let's not mull over the past too much. I don't want to burden you with the accounts of the past. I do have a new proposition for you. I think if you can write about your new experiences, it'll be much easier to publish it, and a lot of people would be interested in it. Still, we have to be very careful about how we do it."

"Get out of my house, please," I said, though it wasn't even my house. I rolled myself back to the window, looking out at the walnut tree, waiting for him to leave.

"I am not sure if you understand me. You cannot really rely on the news from the state TV that much. The climate is really different now and you want to benefit from that. These pro-tests do mean something. They do have an impact. There are different groups within the state that are getting the message. Yes, they just want better business for themselves, but they understand that it requires dialogue. They understand that it is not possible within the existing framework. They acknowledge the need for fundamental change. Now is the moment — a once-in-a-lifetime opportunity to do something meaningful. It will help if people know about what happened to you. It will give everyone a better understanding of the past. There is hope for change. Wasn't that part of what you were trying to achieve? Isn't it our mission as artists to reveal the truth? Don't we all want to change the status quo?"

"Please leave," Tara said this time. "He is still in recovery. He'll think about it later."

He sat there for several minutes, and when none of us said anything, he stood and walked toward the door.

"Nice seeing you two," he said. "I'll be in touch."

Tara followed him to the door. "Thanks for dropping by," she said and shut the door behind him.

•   •   •

We cashed the cheque, and I was able to pay Tara back for the hospital expenses.

"You don't need to do this," she said. "You may need it yourself."

"I'll feel better this way," I said. But I wasn't going to be able to pay her back for everything.

When she was at work, I continued to write.

I wondered if she was going to suggest accepting the Publisher's offer, but she didn't say anything about it. The Publisher called multiple times, but gave up after a couple of weeks. During my breaks from writing, I wheeled myself to the park, or to the back alleys in the surrounding neighbourhood.

Gradually, I was able to go for longer distances, as my hands got stronger.

The closer to downtown I got, the more the unrest became obvious. Police and guards everywhere, many stores closed. People were vigorously searched when entering banks and state buildings.

Burnt tires and shattered glass on sidewalks. Garbage cans pulled out of their place, set on fire, blocking the streets.

Under such circumstances, I had started looking for an apartment. Checking the ads in front of the tall buildings, calling the phone numbers for the superintendents. The money from the book would probably help me pay the rent, and I could go back to copy-editing again to make more.

A superintendent showed me a small studio with built-in shelves, a brownish carpet. It had a window in the kitchen that looked onto the street. Tara came with me the next day to look at it again.

She opened all the closets and cabinets. "It looks okay. But do you think you'll be okay here? It's a bit small," she said.

"Don't you remember our first place? It was smaller than this," I said.

It had been a tiny one-bedroom. We didn't have that much money. I remembered how we had furnished it, searching for every single item at antique markets, wanting it all to be authentic, to be representative of us. We painted the walls different colours. A friend of mine made all our shelves.

We used to make bread and pastries. Cook everything from scratch. So many friends used to come over. What had happened to all those people?

"But don't you want to leave the country?" she asked.

I didn't know why this agitated me. Maybe it felt like she wanted to get rid of me. Or maybe it was about my father's departure. About being left behind. I didn't want to leave, though I didn't have anyone or anything to leave behind other than her.

"There is nowhere else to go," I said.

"Don't you think you should at least talk to someone? You have gone through a lot, and you haven't talked about it."

"I am not sure if talking will do much."

I had wished to talk to her, but never felt I could.

She was biting her lip, but she didn't argue. It was like we had gone back several years, repeating the same frustrated remarks.

"At least promise you'll continue going to your rehabilitation sessions. You can't remain in a wheelchair for the rest of your life."

Several weeks later, I packed up everything with her help. Two suitcases of clothes. Ten boxes of books. A laptop. A couple of pots and plates. I didn't take my desk as it was too big for the new place. Everything else didn't belong to me, or I left it behind.

All of my stuff didn't even fill a small truck.

Tara's parents were there the day I was moving out.

"We're sorry, B," they said. "Let us know if we can help with anything."

•   •   •

In the new apartment, I got a mattress and a much smaller desk. I placed the desk in the kitchen in front of the window.

The apartment looked very empty and I contemplated whether I had to buy some furniture, but I didn't have that much money.

I sat at my desk for many hours every day, moved the words around in the file saved on the memory stick. I added more words. I hid the memory stick in the toilet tank at the end of the day. I added a second lock to the entrance door. I placed a small rug in front of the door. I checked every single ruffle on the rug every time I left home or returned, so I would know if someone had entered the apartment.

After what had happened with the book about my father, I wasn't going to try to publish anything.

No one was going to read what I was writing, but I kept going with it.

At used bookstores, I searched for another copy of *The Book of the Winds*, but no matter how much I looked, I couldn't find one. Booksellers told me they hadn't seen it in many years. I told them about the copy I had found and lost.

"Seems unlikely that you found a copy only a couple of years ago," they said. "It was pulled off the shelves a long time ago." They said this in disbelief, as if I was lying to them.

As for my father's red notebook, I tried to re-create it from my memory. I had read it so many times when on the ship, it wasn't that difficult.

"More scattered riots by the enemies of the people were suppressed today," the state TV announced.

One day I came back home and the apartment door was half-open. The ruffles on the rug had changed.

I called Tara in shock. I had given her a spare key for emergencies, and I wondered whether she had come in to check on me and left the door open.

"Do you still have my key?" I asked her. I heard the rustling sound as she tried to find it.

"Yes, it's here."

I looked around as I was talking to her. Everything seemed untouched, except that some of the books had been taken away, leaving an empty space in the shelves.

"Did you come here today, by any chance?" I asked.

"No. Why are you asking? Is everything all right?"

I checked the bathroom; the memory stick was still in its place.

"Yes," I responded.

"Do you need anything? Do you want me to come over there?" she asked.

"No, I just got disoriented a bit. Everything is all right."

"I meant to call you anyways," she said. "But I can call later if this isn't a good time."

She hadn't called since the day I had left. "No, it's a good time now. What is it?"

"I've had the house on the market for a while. And I finally got an offer. The offer was for less than I was hoping for, but it's understandable, given everything."

"Where are you moving to?" I asked.

"I have a ticket to leave the country in two weeks."

It probably shouldn't have mattered to me, but it did. I found it hard to show any reaction. Had she planned this all along?

"Are you going alone?" I asked.

"Why are you asking?" She sighed.

I didn't know why I asked this or whether it mattered.

"Are you sure you're okay?" she asked.

"Yes," I said. "Will I see you before you leave?"

"Of course. I'll come over to say goodbye," she said. "By the way, my parents said you can call them if you ever need anything when I am gone."

"It's very kind of them."

I was so shocked by the news that I had totally forgotten about the break-in. Only after several hours, I remembered it again and started searching around to see if I might find any surveillance devices hidden anywhere. But I wasn't able to find anything.

Several days later, Tara came to say goodbye. She had brought me the box of our letters.

"I found these for you," she said.

She didn't stay for long and was in a rush to leave.

"My flight is tomorrow and I am not even fully packed," she said. "You have my parents' number? I'll call you once things are settled."

Then we said goodbye. I opened the door. She walked toward the elevator. I waited there and watched her. I listened to the sound of the elevator going down, then rolled my wheelchair to the kitchen and watched her through the window. She got into a cab, the cab started moving, the cab turned onto another street and disappeared.

• • •

I stayed home for several days and read our letters. I left only to go to the corner store downstairs to pick up cans of food and bread. I had put up an ad at the same corner store asking if someone needed tutoring or copy-editing.

"Someone was asking what you look like," the store owner said. "I didn't tell them. I don't know why they need to know that if they have some copy-editing job for you."

"A man or a woman?" I asked.

"A man in his fifties, I think," he said. "Maybe he just recognized your name and knew you from somewhere?"

They called me from the hospital, telling me that I had missed my session the day before and I'd still have to pay for it.

I didn't write for several weeks. The sky was a dark grey, and the streets looked empty. I learned from the TV that a curfew was in place after nine p.m. that week. I switched back to the nature channel and dozed off with the TV on. At night I heard homeless people swearing in the street, the guards taking them away in their vans. Their carts were left on the sidewalks.

Dogs barked in the distance. I couldn't go to sleep.

I hadn't heard anything from Tara since her departure and I wondered if I had to call her parents to ask if she'd arrived safely.

The next time I left the apartment was to go to my hospital appointment.

"Where is your caretaker today?" the technician asked.

"She's gone," I said.

She became quiet after that and didn't say anything. We just continued with my exercises.

"You have made a lot of progress," she said. "Try to walk with your walker an hour a day at least."

On my way back to the apartment, people had gathered at an entrance to a recently shut-down museum and were chanting slogans against the state. The guards hadn't arrived at the scene yet.

A man was standing with a container of gasoline in his hand at the top of the stairs.

"Leave us," he screamed before he poured the gasoline on himself.

The audience clapped as he did this.

I rolled my wheelchair away from the scene, trying to make my way back to the apartment. The man was still standing, shivering, and I heard sirens and the roar of the guards' motorcycles.

As I turned onto another street, I noticed two bearded men running after me. I wheeled as fast as I could. I considered entering a grocery store, where people might help me, but then changed my mind and continued on the crowded sidewalk, then cut down through the middle of the street. The cars slammed to a stop only a metre away from me. The drivers honked at me.

"Are you fucking crazy?" they shouted.

When I got to the other side of the street, the men were still following me. I could still hear their heavy breathing. I expected them to stop and detain me or ask me for my ID, which would lead to the same thing, given my history, given that I was escaping from them, but they just passed me by. They might have been running from the scene themselves.

I changed my direction and took another route toward home. After a while, I looked around again and couldn't see anything abnormal. I slowed down, then stopped at a park. I remembered that I didn't have anything at home and needed to buy something to eat.

As I was watching a woman push a stroller around the park, she turned and looked back, and for a moment I thought that it was the informant from the rig. I pushed my wheelchair toward her, but when I got closer, I saw it wasn't her.

The woman looked at me in shock and sped up her steps. The baby started to cry with the sudden movement of the stroller.

. . .

I practised walking inside the apartment. Once, as I was practising, I fell to the floor and couldn't make my way back to my
wheelchair. I stayed like that for many hours, not knowing
what to do. It became dark and I was very hungry, but given
the curfew, even if I had called someone, they wouldn't have
been able to do anything. I couldn't control my urine. I slept
on the floor, cold, stiff, and wet, then woke and waited for the
sun to rise. I crawled toward my phone, contemplating who to
call, and ended up calling Tara's father.

He came after an hour. He had the key that I had left with
Tara and was able to enter the apartment. He brought some
breakfast and fruits. He lifted me and helped me get back into
my wheelchair.

I was able to go to the bathroom and change afterward. The
side that I had fallen on hurt more.

"Do you want to go to the emergency room? Are you sure
you haven't hurt yourself?"

"I think it's just a bruise. I only fell on my side."

He'd rolled up the wet rug and left it by the door. But he
didn't say anything about it.

I ate the food he had brought and took some painkillers.

"I am so sorry to put you to trouble," I said.

"Hopefully this won't happen again, but please call earlier next
time if it does," he said. "You've been in pain for many hours."

"How's Tara?" I asked.

"She's good — she arrived there safely, but it takes a while
to settle, as you can imagine. B, forgive me for asking, but do
you have enough money? Would you like to stay with us for a
few days, until you're better?"

I told him that I was feeling stronger and this had been just an accident. I told him I had enough money and I was trying to take on more editing jobs. Worst case, I could always apply for an administrative job.

"Let me know if you need any help with that," he said. "As you know, I know a lot of people. I've got to go now. Please be careful — it's unsafe out there. Don't go out unless you have to. Don't carry any cash or anything valuable. You don't know which you should be more afraid of: the guards or the hungry people. A friend of mine was mugged two days ago."

• • •

The curfew continued. I gradually went back to writing. I kept practising with my walker and I was able to walk more steadily. A week later, someone delivered the cleaned rug to my door. I tried to avoid the crowds when I had to go for my hospital appointments.

Tara called me several days later. "Sorry, I wasn't able to call earlier. Took me a while to get things going," she said. "How are you, B? Are you better?"

"Yes, much better now," I said. I wondered whether her father had told her about what had happened.

"How are things there?" I asked.

"Things are moving forward slowly — I rented an apartment. It's not bad, same size as yours. I'm looking for a job now.

"This is my new number, by the way," she said, then we said goodbye.

The next time I went to the corner store, the owner had a bandage on his head. He said that he had been attacked for a can of tuna, his supplies were running low, and he was thinking of shutting down for a while.

"If you haven't already stocked up, you might consider
doing so. Things are only going to get worse."

• • •

On the streets, I kept mistaking someone else for the informant
from the rig. Each time she would turn and I would realize that
it wasn't actually her.

I remembered her face when we lost each other in the ocean
during the rain. Her short hair and her sharp cheekbones.

Had it been guilt that had made her want to help me? Or
had our escape from the ship been orchestrated, like other
events?

Then I saw her in the front row of a crowd, chanting slogans. She was holding a placard with a message I couldn't read.
I followed the crowd, trying to push my way through to get to
her. More and more people joined the protesters. I looked back
and I couldn't see how far the crowd continued.

We entered a wide uphill street with pine trees on both
sides. It became harder for me to keep up with the crowd.
Even uphill I couldn't see where the crowd ended. I hadn't
ever seen so many people walking together, with no signs of
guards.

I pushed forward, trying to follow the white placard. She
turned and for a moment, I could see her face. Her hair had
grown long again. It was really her. I tried to wave from my
wheelchair, but she didn't see me.

The crowd segregated into two different streets and I was
carried along into one of them. Soon after, clouds of tear gas

spread, burning my eyes. The protestors covered their faces with clothes, ran around, and dispersed.

A man removed his shirt and lit it on fire to make a torch. Several men had captured a guard and were kicking him in the abdomen. The guard's respirator had fallen off his face. He looked small and fragile. He was probably not even twenty. His mouth was filled with blood.

"He is just a kid," an older woman told the men. "Stop this. You should be ashamed of yourselves."

I made my way out of the crowd, coughing through the smoke and fog.

. . .

I never saw her again after that, though several other times on the street I mistook someone else for her. I wasn't fully sure if she had saved my life on the ship, or if they'd have let me go at some point, anyway. At least I knew she was alive. I didn't have any leads to search for her.

I dreamed I received a letter that asked me to show up for interrogations concerning what I was writing now.

The demonstrations became sparser as the guards' violence increased, until they completely died down.

The aisles of the grocery stores filled with food again.

The owner of the corner store reopened his shop.

There were no more calls from Tara. Her father helped me with getting some new copy-editing assignments. He told me that Tara was doing well.

The Publisher called me to say things had changed for the worse again, but he was interested in discussing a new opportunity with me.

I never heard anything back from the Editor, just that he had managed to escape the country.

When the winter arrived, I was able to walk with my walker outside.

Dogs ran around happily, splattering the snow.

Icicles hung from gutters.

The snow covered the dried grass.

I followed the footprints in the snow.

ACKNOWLEDGEMENTS

Thanks to Peter Markus, Zach Davidson, and Ian Mallov for the encouragement and feedback on multiple versions of the book

Thanks to Kwame Scott Fraser, Russell Smith, Erin Pinksen, Laura Boyle, and the rest of the team at Dundurn Press

Thanks to Akin Akinwumi, my agent

Thanks to Blake Butler, Amina Cain, Brandon Hobson, and Bud Smith for offering their generous words and support of this work

Thanks to the Ontario Arts Council for their generous financial support

To Sara

To my parents

To Bashu and Louli, the cutest companions

ABOUT THE AUTHOR

Babak Lakghomi is the author of the novella *Floating Notes*. His writing has appeared in *American Short Fiction*, *NOON*, *Ninth Letter*, *New York Tyrant*, and the *Adroit Journal*, among other places, and has been translated into Italian and Farsi. Babak was born in Tehran, Iran, and currently lives and writes in Toronto.